MURDER FOLLOWS MONEY

A Liz Sullivan Mystery

Lora Roberts

FAWCETT • NEW YORK

A Fawcett Book
Published by The Ballantine Publishing Group

www.randomhouse.com/BB/

Library of Congress Card Number: 99-91915

ISBN 0-449-00539-9

Manufactured in the United States of America

First Edition: May 2000

10   9   8   7   6   5   4   3   2   1

ACKNOWLEDGMENTS

I'd like to thank Kathy Goldmark for giving me a glimpse of the media escort's world. Any inaccuracies are mine, either outright mistakes or plot exigencies. I'd also like to thank Phyllis Malpas, toxicologist and vet, for her knowledgeable assistance. All characters herein are fictional and bear no resemblance to any real person, living or dead.

I raise my wineglass to three fine women, wonderful traveling companions, and excellent mystery writers: Jonnie Jacobs, Lee Harris, and Valerie Wolzien, aka Nuns, Mothers and Others.

1

I stood at a gate in the San Francisco Airport, slightly behind Judi Kershay, my employer of the moment. I was holding a copy of Hannah Couch's latest book on entertaining, in which she not only told how to bring home the bacon and cook it up in a pan, but how to serve it beautifully to thirty people.

I was not fond of doing temporary work, but writing freelance magazine articles, my usual way of earning money, could be uncertain. Liz Sullivan was by no means an easily recognized name among magazine editors, although my pieces had been published in *Women's World*, *Organic Gardening*, and even once, the pinnacle of my career, *Smithsonian*. After tasting those lofty heights, I'd been sending my stuff to more selective markets than *Grit* and *True Confessions*, former sources of small but steady money. I had expenses to meet, and no income with which to meet them. At such times, I dove into the pool of temporary workers that populated the San Francisco Bay Area.

Not five hours previously, I had been peacefully copying travel vouchers and answering telephones in the San Mateo office of Kershay-Pederson Media Alliance, filling in for a flu-stricken receptionist. January was a good month for temp work because so many people were home sick with flu and colds and general post-holiday malaise.

I had worked at Kershay-Pederson for two days, while the receptionist phoned every three or four hours to moan about how sick she was and ask if I needed help. Her job had been relatively simple, as January was also a slack time for book promotions, the firm's mainstay.

That morning, Irene Pederson had called in sick. And then another call, one that caused Judi Kershay to erupt from her office.

"Quick. Call Maria. Maybe she hasn't left yet."

I found Maria on the list of drivers who escorted authors around to bookstores and talk shows. Her answering machine assured me that she'd return my call at the earliest possible time.

"Not her home number. Isn't her cell-phone number there?"

I tried the next number. It rang a few times, and then a staticky voice said, "This is Maria Lopez."

"Judi Kershay for you." I handed the receiver to Judi, but I didn't go back to filing right away. The drama enacted in front of me was too compelling.

"Maria, did you already pick up Shirley Climo?" Judi barely waited for an answer. "So it's not too late. I'll get someone else for her. I need you to drive Hannah Couch. She's arriving"—Judi looked at her watch—"in less than two hours."

I could hear Maria's reaction to that. "I know she can be difficult—" Judi's voice was placating. "That's why we have the bonus for driving her."

More squawking. "But, Maria—" Judi listened intently. "Yes, I know. I know. Forget it. I understand." She handed the receiver back to me and rubbed the vertical lines that had formed between her eyebrows. "I didn't think she would. And Susan is out sick, Leona is on vacation, even poor Irene is sick, and Hannah can't stand me."

"Excuse me." I cleared my throat. "Are we talking about *the* Hannah Couch? The one with all the books, and the magazine, and the TV show?"

"That's the one." Judi looked at me, her eyes narrowed. "Do you drive, Liz? Of course you do, you live in Palo Alto."

"I have a car—a '69 VW microbus," I replied promptly. "But I took the train today."

"Do you know your way around the City?"

"Tolerably well." I had driven around San Francisco, which in an old car with a clutch is a bit of a challenge. And I had maps, lots of maps. My ostensible reason for joining the Triple A was the age of my bus, which any moment might break down in ways I was unable to fix. Really, however, I joined to get as many maps as I want.

"Would you like to upgrade your position? You can be Hannah's media escort."

I blinked. "Me? Don't you need social graces for that kind of thing?"

Judi smiled grimly. "In Hannah's case, you just need thick skin. She doesn't mince words when she's dissatisfied, and believe me, it takes a lot to satisfy her. Last time she was here, I worked with her myself because none of the available drivers would take her on again, even with the bonus. She and I . . . didn't get along." Her lips closed tightly.

"Does she use whips and chains? Water torture? What's so bad?" I pictured Hannah Couch as she appeared on the covers of countless books—*Hannah Cooks Italian*,

3

Hannah Cooks French, *Hannah Cooks Light*. She was always beaming a motherly smile, her slightly plump body encased in a sparkling white apron, her silvery hair drawn back in a bun, with a halo of curls around her face. "She looks so nice."

"She is totally obsessive about the details, not just for her books, but for every appearance she does. Maybe that's why she's so successful. At any rate, she likes her entourage to be at her beck and call, do exactly what they're told, and not challenge her authority in any way. Do you think you could do that?"

I thought it would be hard. I was used to being in charge myself, even though I only had myself to be in charge of, and my dog Barker. Barker had not liked being left home alone the previous two days. My neighbor and very good friend Paul Drake had come home at lunchtime to let him out for a while, but even so he'd greeted me in the evening with a reproachful air. I knew Paul would take care of him if my job involved longer hours. But neither of them would be happy.

"What kind of commitment are we talking about here?"

Judi gave me an approving look. "I like a person who thinks things through before she jumps in. You would pick up Hannah and whatever entourage she brings along at the airport in"—she glanced at her watch—"one hour and fifty minutes. Her publisher will provide a limo, so you don't have to actually drive. You just make sure she gets to all her events on time; I'll give you a list as soon as her publicist faxes it to me. You get her whatever she needs, whether that's toiletries or tortillas for a cooking demonstration. You make sure everything at the hotel is okay and if it's not, switch her rooms. You prep her for the appearances."

"You mean, makeup and stuff?" My voice came out a high-pitched squeak. "I don't know anything about that."

Judi laughed. "Not makeup. Prep her as in remind her that Ronn Owens likes his guests to be funny, and Fanci-Foods Marketplace expects a cooking demonstration when she appears there, and stuff like that."

"I don't know anything about that, either." I shook my head. "I don't think I'm woman enough for this job, Judi."

"You could do it, Liz. I've noticed you're a quick study. You mastered the fax machine, didn't you?"

"How did you know I'd never faxed before?"

"Actually, I didn't." She gave me a quizzical look. "I just thought you'd never used that particular fax, which is all you said about it. So you are a quick study. You'd get the hang of it in no time. And did I mention the bonus?" She leaned closer. "Of course the pay for an escort is better than the receptionist right off the bat. Then we offer a hundred-dollar-a-day bonus because Hannah is so difficult. I can arrange to pay that directly to you; the temp agency doesn't have to know about it. In fact, if you want, I can just hire you as one of my workers and you can ditch the temp agency altogether."

"Great. I'll take it." My mouth said those words though my brain still had major doubts. But my reason for doing temp work was to pay my property taxes and homeowners insurance; I didn't like dipping into my savings for anything short of major catastrophe, and my wee retirement account was sacrosanct. It would be nice to pile up a real cushion, as long as I had to do temp work

5

anyway. The whole economy of Silicon Valley was booming in a major way, causing an acute shortage of worker bees. Even my primitive office skills were in demand. The agency with which I was registered found me troublesome, but lately they were desperate, and their desperation coincided with my need. That fortunate alignment of planets might not happen again; it was up to me to make hay while the temporary sun shone.

And that was how I came to be standing at the airport, waiting for Hannah Couch—*the* Hannah Couch—and her entourage to deplane. I carried a copy of *Hannah Hosts Brunch* because Judi said that was better than holding up a sign with a celebrity's easily recognizable name on it, which might cause a bit of rumpus at the airport gate.

"But everyone will recognize her anyway. Even I would recognize her."

"You might be surprised," she said cryptically. "I'll stay around until after she's deplaned, so I will know her if you don't. But then I have to cut out, because she hates me, and she'll remember that about five minutes after I say hello."

"If she hates you, why did she call you at the last minute like this? Aren't there other companies that do this?"

Judi shrugged. "She's been through a lot of us already. And perhaps she hates them more, I don't know. I wouldn't even have taken the job, but her publisher sends a lot of work our way, and I didn't want that to stop. It's only a few days. You can put up with aggravation until Friday, right?"

I cleared my throat. "I'm not known for being tactful, Judi. In fact, the reverse."

She didn't look fazed. "Look, the only thing that matters is to do it. I told the publicist we hadn't had time to prep. She understands we're doing them a favor by taking this on at the last minute. Even if it's a disaster, we've come out ahead. And what could go wrong in such a short time?"

"Why is it the last minute? Aren't these things usually planned out very carefully in advance?"

Judi snorted with laughter. Since I had agreed to take on escorting Hannah Couch, her mood had lightened considerably. "The publicist didn't say, but evidently Hannah had a bit of a tantrum. It's been known to happen."

I swallowed. "What if that happens to me?"

"She won't have any media escort." Judi put a hand on my shoulder. "Relax. Just do the best you can. She'll have other people to vent on. She might even be nice to you. One of our drivers thinks she's just wonderful, but that woman is out of town until next month."

So we ended up at the airport. I took a deep breath and tried to remember what Judi had been drilling into me for the past hour. Hannah Couch would have an entourage. Her personal assistant would go with her everywhere. She might bring a food stylist, which would let me off the hook in that department. I hadn't known until then that food could be styled. She might also bring a photographer if she wanted to document a significant part of her tour for her magazine, *Hannah's Home*. Likewise a reporter or writer to record her pithy words and sayings.

Caught up in the whole thing by then, I found myself on the verge of offering my services as writer. Just in time, I managed to remember one of Liz Sullivan's Rules for Better Living: Never volunteer before you know what you're getting into. I believe it's Rule No. 37. I've kind of lost count since my life's taken a turn for the better in the last year or so.

Having never flown anywhere, I found just being in the airport exotic. I'd been there a few times to pick up my niece Amy and drop her off again, and done the same service for Paul Drake.

My thoughts tended to drift toward Paul lately. We had been friends for a couple of years, but in the past few months we'd gotten much closer. I still had a few reservations about our relationship, but mostly it had been very positive. In fact, if I didn't stop thinking about him while I was supposed to be working, I'd totally lose track of my job.

Uniformed people milled around the tunnel-like opening that led to the plane. Judi Kershay straightened and took a deep breath, closing her eyes briefly in what I assumed was prayer. I held the copy of Hannah's new book more prominently. Looking around at smartly uniformed chauffeurs, I hoped my low-key appearance wouldn't be held against me. My usual thrift-shop office wear consisted of a twill skirt, inexpertly altered by my own loving hands, as the previous owner had been both taller and broader than I, and a white shirt. The thick-soled black loafers had come from Amy, who'd left them at my house after her last visit, complaining that they pinched her toes. They fit me okay, and were even comfortable, but the heavy lug soles made me feel like an escapee from an orthopedic ward.

A clot of people swept toward us. A middle-aged woman, salt-and-pepper hair pulled back severely from her unsmiling face, was in the center of the group. Could that be Hannah Couch? She bore a faint resemblance to the dimply, perfectly coiffed woman who popped up regularly on the covers of magazines at the grocery store checkout. Judi Kershay waved, and I held up the book. The woman moved toward us, trailing her group.

Judi stepped forward. "Hannah. How nice to see you again."

Hannah bestowed an automatic smile on her. "Lovely to be back in San Francisco." The smile faded. "Is it Judi?"

"Yes. Fancy you remembering my name." Judi's voice was sweet, but an acid undertone came through. "I'm just here to introduce your escort. Then I must run." She pulled me forward. "This is Liz. She'll be taking care of you while you're in San Francisco."

"Nice to meet you." I gulped and stuck out my hand. I'd never been so close to a famous person before.

Hannah's brown eyes sized me up coolly as she made brief contact with my hand. "Liz. I'm sure we'll work well together."

"I hope so." I spoke to her back. She had already turned away.

Judi winked at me. "Well, I'll be running along. Keep in touch, Liz."

I remembered the cell phone in my knapsack, which had been colonized by so much of Judi's stuff that it was more like her briefcase now. It held a sheaf of papers, the cell phone, petty cash for incidentals, and cab fare to the train station for me whenever I was released from duty that day. The next day I would have to drive from Palo Alto to the City and arrive by seven A.M. That meant an early start at six A.M.; it always takes longer in my elderly bus.

9

Judi walked away, and I watched her, feeling adrift and, for some reason, apprehensive. But I would shake it off. After all, it was only until Friday. What could go wrong in such a short time?

2

A sharp tap on my shoulder returned my attention to the task at hand. One of the members of Hannah's group, a woman with a lined face and improbable auburn hair, wearing sweats and running shoes, looked at me through narrowed gray eyes.

"Shouldn't you be getting the bags?"

"Yes, of course." I remembered my instructions. "I'll show you where the limo is waiting, then bring the bags out."

I led them down the corridor, feeling as if I was in one of those movies where the purposeful group marches toward a common goal. The scowling woman walked beside Hannah, speaking in her ear in a low voice. A tall, loose-jointed young man ambled up beside me. His mop of dark hair caught red highlights from the light. His expression was one of total detachment. He had a leather duffel slung over his shoulder, and carried a silvery attaché case. I put him down as photographer.

"I've never been to San Francisco before," he offered. "Is it far to the baggage claim?"

"It's a pretty good ways." I glanced at him. "My name is Liz."

"I'm Don Wozjicki." He smiled, at least I think it was

a smile. His face mostly stayed in a deadpan expression. "No one told you our names," he went on. "Naomi Matthews is the bossy one." I suppressed a smile at the accuracy of that description. "And Kim's hiding behind you." He reached around and pulled a young woman forward. She was slight as a gazelle, with shy, startled eyes beneath a mop of red hair. She gave me a fleeting smile, but said nothing. "That's us," Don finished, lapsing into silence.

I am not particularly outgoing, but I found myself wanting to set Kim at ease.

"I'm Liz." I smiled at her. "Have you all been on the road long?"

She glanced behind her. Naomi was bent protectively over Hannah Couch; Don appeared to be in his own world as he slouched along.

"It seems like forever," the young woman said, "but this is only our second stop. And the first one didn't count, according to Naomi."

"Are you the food stylist?" I asked hopefully.

"Yes." Kim stared at her feet on the escalator. "Although we understood that you would do the shopping and help prep the food."

"Yeah, well, I will, if I can figure out how to do it."

Kim caught her breath. "Oh, dear." She looked at the two behind us again. "Naomi will be angry. She specifically asked for an escort experienced with food preparation."

"I'll do my best." I shrugged, trying to throw off the feeling of impending doom—my doom. This job paid better than anything I'd ever done before, if I didn't get fired on the first day. But there were other jobs, and firing might be merciful. I was just sorry for Judi Kershay if things didn't work out. "Is Naomi the dragon woman?"

Kim was really striking when she smiled. I wondered why the lanky photographer wasn't paying more attention to her.

"That's Naomi. She's been with Hannah since they first opened a restaurant together—'Beaned in Boston.' It's famous. Have you heard of it?"

"Not really. Never been to the East Coast." Or much of anywhere, save for my hometown of Denver, a place I thought of as overfull of my less-than-happy family and a host of unpleasant memories. I wouldn't return there anytime soon, and had no plans to go anywhere else, or money to get there. Perhaps it was the airport ambience, but wanderlust stirred in my soul, and it took the forcible reminder of my depleted bank account to tamp it down.

Kim's smile faded. "That's where I worked. My uncle Tony managed it."

"A family thing, was it?"

"Yes, actually. Naomi is my aunt, his sister. Uncle Tony had a heart attack and died last month. I miss him." Kim sighed. "We had such fun at the restaurant. It's a take-out place, you know—lots of really neat dishes and people take them home to heat up. I loved assembling the meals for people. I could just see them putting the food on nice plates, maybe lighting candles because they had time to fix up a little instead of cooking. And Uncle Tony and the other staff there were all so nice." She sighed again.

"I'm sorry about your uncle."

"Hmm?" Kim came back from her daydream. "It's really because of him that I'm here. Aunt Naomi came in to check things out a couple of days before Uncle Tony's attack, and told him they had just learned their food stylist took another job. She was really steamed, and she's nasty when she's mad. Uncle Tony made some comment

13

like, 'Oh, Kim could do as good a job as that girl did.' We all laughed, but after his death, Naomi just—snapped me up."

"Like a crocodile," I suggested.

Kim's smile was perfunctory. "It's been awful. I didn't know anything to begin with. I still don't know much. I think she only keeps me around because she loves to complain and I always do something to complain about."

"Well, tell me what you want me to do and I'll make a few mistakes. She can complain at me for a while."

We reached the baggage-claim area. The bags for Hannah's flight hadn't come up yet. I turned to watch Hannah and Naomi approach. "Why don't I take you out to the limo?" I suggested to them. "Then I can wait for your bags."

"Don will stay here and help," Naomi decreed. "You may as well stay too, Kim." She rummaged in her big shoulder bag. "Here are the claim checks. Be as quick as you can. Hannah needs to get to her hotel for a rest."

"I'm fine, Naomi." Hannah looked bored by the commotion. "Where *is* the car?"

We had to wait for a few moments outside the door until the right limousine hove into view. I hoisted Hannah's book in the air, as Judi had told me to, and soon one of the big vehicles pulled over. Naomi tucked Hannah tenderly into the back while I spoke to the driver. He wasn't allowed to park at the curb, but promised to circle until we emerged with the baggage.

I joined Don and Kim at the baggage claim. With Hannah and Naomi out of the way, Kim was perceptibly more relaxed.

"So, Don, you've never been here before. What about you, Kim?"

"Never." She glanced around the airport. "From here it doesn't look much different from Boston."

"Well, I've never been to Boston. But maybe the weather's better here in January."

"Couldn't be worse." Don spoke around the wad of chewing gum he'd crammed in his mouth.

"Don's from Florida," Kim explained. "He's been complaining about our New England winters ever since Naomi hired him." She looked up at him with her wistful smile. "Don't you love the skiing and sledding? And walking in the crisp, frosty air? I do."

He smiled faintly at her, then, with a movement much faster than I'd expected from him, had a camera in his hand and was taking her picture. "Couldn't resist," he said around the gum, flicking the tip of her nose with a careless finger. "You're cute when you think about cold weather."

He turned away, but not before I'd glimpsed the warmth at the back of his teasing smile.

Kim shrugged. "He treats me like I was his kid sister," she whispered to me, looking at Don's back with an exasperated expression. "Don't you think he's cute, Liz?"

"He's good-looking if you like that lanky style."

"Right. He's too lanky for me." Kim tossed her head. "Do you have a boyfriend at home?"

She looked at her nails, blushing. "A couple of boys take me out. They're nice and all. But Don's, like, a *man*."

"Luggage is up," the *man* called out just then. "Get a-moving, ladies."

I got a baggage cart and we stacked some big plastic crates on it. "The cooking supplies," Kim said. "Some

15

nice dishes. Hannah doesn't take chances. She brings everything she might need for a demonstration."

Don hefted a couple of big duffel bags. "What's in these?"

Kim thought. "I believe they have linens. Maybe some of Naomi's makeup stuff." She turned to me. "Naomi does all the personal things for Hannah—gets her ready for appearances and things like that."

"Thank God," I muttered. "And these must be Hannah's." The suitcases were large, elegant leather and tapestry, with wheels.

"One's Hannah's, the other's Naomi's. And they have these littler ones too." Kim draped smaller bags around the larger ones, like saddlebags on mules. "And this is mine." She found a place on the luggage cart for a battered old suitcase. "This belongs to my folks," she said, catching my eye. "Nobody travels much in my family."

Don had another duffel bag, which he swung onto his shoulder, balancing the camera case and small duffel he already carried. We draped the big duffels on top of the crates on the luggage cart and Don wheeled it, listing precariously, out the doors, while Kim and I followed with the more elegant bits. Considering that they were on a multicity tour, I guessed it wasn't that much luggage, but it sure made for a lot of schlepping. I was thankful that after we got it into the hotel, I wouldn't have to wrassle with it again until Friday.

The limo was lurking for us when we lurched through the doors. The driver helped Don stow luggage, hindered by Naomi's demands to keep one piece with her. Don sat up front, and Kim and I crawled into the middle seat in back, facing Hannah and Naomi.

The limo was incredibly plush, the fanciest car by far

that I had ever been in, including my sister's lavishly appointed sport utility vehicle. The driver pulled away, and we four women sat silently, staring at each other.

I cleared my throat, breaking the silence. "What's your favorite thing about San Francisco, Ms. Couch?" This inane remark popped out, and was left unanswered for a minute. I could feel those cold eyes on me.

"What is your name again?" Her voice, clear and mellifluous, gave the lie to that salt-and-pepper hair. I wondered why she didn't dye it.

"Liz Sullivan."

"Have you acted as an escort before?"

"My first time." I couldn't help myself. I smiled at her as we pulled onto the highway. "Please be gentle."

She was taken aback. "Well, Ms. Sullivan," she said finally, "do you know what to do? As my media escort, you should be telling me something about the places I'm scheduled to be."

"Right." I swung my knapsack around and got out the first of several file folders Judi Kershay had pressed on me. "We should be at the hotel in another half hour, barring bad traffic," I began in my most official voice. "By the way, we're now driving past San Bruno Mountain, home of the rare blue checkerspot butterfly."

Kim pressed her nose against the glass, as if the butterfly was hanging around the freeway waiting to show its stuff. Naomi looked bored. Hannah stared at me stolidly.

"At the hotel, you'll have an hour or so to freshen up. Then the *San Francisco Chronicle* food and entertainment editor is coming to interview you, about three P.M."

"Is that Randy Nevis?" Now the disapproval in her voice was marked. She turned to Naomi. "I thought I made it clear I wouldn't talk to him again."

17

"Just this once," Naomi said soothingly. "There's really no way to get out of talking to the *Chronicle*. It's the major newspaper in this area."

"Actually," I said, clearing my throat, "The *San Jose Mercury News* is considered to outclass the *Chronicle*, at least by the Silicon Valley types."

Hannah looked at Naomi, triumphant. "See?" She turned to me. "When am I speaking with the *Mercury News*?"

"I don't know that you are." I shuffled frantically through the papers I held. "Perhaps they didn't ask for an interview, or your publicist didn't let them know you'd be in the area."

"Or they just don't have the readership to matter," Naomi sniffed. Her look at me could have cut through steel.

"Set it up," Hannah ordered. She didn't look at Naomi or me, and I was at a loss to know who was supposed to follow this command. Naomi sat back in her seat, two spots of color burning on her cheeks, her lips pressed together. The look she darted to Hannah was anything but worshipful; I could have sworn there was real enmity in it.

Her voice held a challenge when she spoke. "Will the *Chronicle* bring a photographer? If so, an hour isn't long enough. You'll have to put them off."

The first major fly in my oatmeal. Hastily I consulted the sheaf of papers Judi Kershay had given me. "It looks like their photographer is going to meet you later, at the demonstration you'll do for *Live at Five*, the talk show on Channel Six. The *Chronicle* wants action shots."

Naomi considered this narrowly before nodding. I breathed a sigh of relief.

I cleared my throat and went on. "*Live at Five* is a news-magazine format. You won't go on until five-fifteen or so, but leaving for the studio at four gives you time for makeup and to get the demonstration area set up."

"Is there anything else this evening?" Hannah pressed her fingers against her eyes. "I was hoping for an early night."

I glanced at the schedule again. "Says here you'll be the guest chef at the gala premiere of the new FanciFoods Marketplace in Pacific Heights at seven-thirty."

"What is that, a grocery store?" Naomi again, her dander up. "They're going to drag us out to a grocery store? Who do they think we are?"

"FanciFoods is like this temple to food. They have a cooking school and cookbook section and it's all very upscale. And only Hannah is mentioned, so maybe you don't have to go, Naomi."

Hannah snorted, and when I looked at her, she was smiling, though it wasn't the kind of smile you want directed at you. "Right, Naomi. You can tuck up and get some rest. I remember that I did say I would do a demonstration for them."

It was starting to make me feel queasy to read in the car, especially sitting backward. I wondered if it would be against the rules to just hand the papers to Hannah and let her read them for herself.

Luckily Kim created a diversion. "What are we demonstrating?"

"We're cooking, Kim," Naomi said, her voice heavily sarcastic. "It's why we're here. We've written a cookbook."

Hannah ignored Naomi's dig and Kim's stricken face. "I want to do two different things. For the market thing, we'll make the *huevos rancheros* casserole. I'll need hand-made tortillas. Free-range eggs. Fresh tomatoes for the salsa. Good chorizo. Make sure you get decent tomatoes."

I had to look out the window of the limo to see if it was still January. From the assurance in Hannah's voice, it might well have been July, or we might have been transported to Oaxaca, where excellent tomatoes would be piled right beside the door to her hotel room. "I'll do my best, but good tomatoes in January are hard to find."

Hannah and Naomi both looked at me as if I'd suddenly started doing a bump-and-grind routine. Kim dug her elbow into my side. "But I'm sure I can find some," I added hastily.

"See that you do. And avocados, not overripe or too hard, just right. Limes. Sour cream. I brought my own epazote, but I'll need fresh cilantro. Garlic, onions—I prefer the white ones, and make sure they're more flat than pointed."

I was scribbling all this down on the schedule. And cursing Judi Kershay. Where would I find all this perfect produce in the City in January? I didn't know where to shop there. And when was I going to get out to do it? I was supposed to be on hand during the newspaper interview to act as doorkeeper, according to Judi. Fetch everyone drinks when they needed them. Keep uninvited people out. Between the interview and leaving for Channel 6 was about twenty minutes. I wouldn't even be able to find a produce market in that length of time, let alone make careful choices.

Naomi had to put in her two cents' worth. "What about the fruit? Weren't you going to build that two-tier fruit compote?"

"Oh, yes." Hannah twinkled her fingers, dismissing

any effort it might take on my part to fulfill her requests. "I'll need at least two ripe pineapples, several mangoes, a dozen kiwis, a couple of bunches of red grapes. The grapes should be frosted."

I gulped. Kim dug her elbow into my side again. When I looked at her, she winked and nodded. I took this to mean that she could frost grapes.

"What about the TV show? They want a demonstration too, don't they?" Naomi had her own notebook out, though she jotted one thing for every ten items I wrote down.

"I think I'll do *crêpes suzette*. It will be an excellent opportunity to demonstrate my new crepe maker. And a TV audience is a better place to push a new product, don't you think, Naomi?" Hannah's voice was sweet, but with a kind of triumph in it.

Naomi gasped. "Don't you mean *my* new crepe maker? I didn't know that was out of production yet. I haven't gotten my milestone payment."

"It's my new crepe maker." A note of steel entered Hannah's voice. "You used my idea for your prototype. And anyway, I've refined it further for production. And my attorneys went through your contract, dear. It specifically says that any devices or inventions you create while in my employment belong to me."

A hushed silence filled the car, the kind of silence that comes before a howling thunderstorm. Kim looked frightened. I wished I was sitting with the driver, blissfully unaware of the gamesmanship going on in the back.

Naomi looked at Hannah with pure hate in her eyes. It gave me the shivers to see it. "You're an evil bitch," she said finally, her voice flat with suppressed fury. "We had an agreement."

"You mean, you tried to hold me up." Hannah shook her head in crocodile sorrow. "After all the years we've been together, after all the profit you've derived from our association, you try to stick it to me. I was shocked, Naomi. To take my idea and try to sell it back to me. That truly takes a kind of hubris I know nothing about."

"It was all my work." Naomi stopped holding back her anger. Her face was inches from Hannah's; her eyes were wild, and her thin lips were pulled away from her teeth like an animal going in for the kill. "You can't just steal it like that. You'll hear from my lawyers!"

"By all means." Hannah didn't seem the least discommoded by Naomi's tirade. "As my dear husband used to say, let the lawyers talk to each other. If we're still to be working together, we'll have to have a good relationship. I couldn't have an associate around who didn't support my goals. Morton used to say, 'If we don't hang together, we'll hang separately.' "

Naomi took a couple of deep breaths and let the implied threat sink in. "Yes, I remember Morton saying those boring things before he . . . died. So unexpected, wasn't it? Some kind of gastrointestinal thing. Of course, it wouldn't be something you cooked for him. For one thing, you rarely cooked at home anymore then. And of course you wouldn't have put the wrong kind of mushrooms in the ragout, or the wrong kind of flowers in the salad." She sighed gustily. "It's sad, though. One minute he was alive, the next he was dead. And you got all his money."

It was Hannah's turn to look venomous. She clamped her lips together tightly. She didn't answer Naomi's not-so-thinly veiled accusation. Instead she looked at her peons, Kim and me.

"You'll need to get the crepe batter made first thing when we get to the hotel, or it won't have settled long enough to work well by five."

It wasn't clear to me if she was speaking to Kim or to me.

"I'll get the eggs and milk somehow. Didn't we bring flour and baking powder and that stuff?" Kim looked nervous again.

"We have staples in one of the crates." Hannah moved on to another topic, seeming revitalized by her run-in with Naomi. "What's on the table tomorrow?"

"A radio talk show, very early. Seven A.M."

"At least I don't have to get dressed. I presume they're doing a feed from the hotel suite."

It didn't say on the schedule. I made yet another note. Judi Kershay would get a very long phone call from me at the first opportunity.

"Ooo, look." Kim was craning around to see out the front of the limo. "It's like Oz or something!"

We had rounded Hospital Curve on 101, and San Francisco was spread out in front of us, from the ridiculous excesses of the Marriott to the gleaming towers of the downtown financial concerns. The hills were covered with buildings—the little boxes of the folk song, though if you tried to buy one, you'd find out how much ticky-tacky costs these days. In the distance, blue water sparkled.

"It's so cute! Like a toy city." Kim was entranced.

Hannah dismissed the view with a cursory "Very nice."

But Naomi seemed particularly struck. She stared out the window and whispered to herself, "San Francisco." Her gaze at the buildings was almost gloating.

23

3

OF course commercial royalty like Hannah Couch would not stay at just any hotel. She was booked at one of the queen hotels of the city. An attendant dripping with gold braid leaped to open the doors of the limo when we pulled up. The masses of luggage were tenderly put on a gold cart and wheeled inside. We made quite a progress through the lobby. Naomi gestured at me, and at first I didn't understand what she meant. Then I realized that it was my job to go to the desk to pick up the room keys.

I have stayed in motels before. The procedure would be similar, I thought. I was wrong.

The woman behind the desk wore a suit and looked formidably impeccable. In my thrift-shop skirt and blouse, I felt totally out of place in this temple of sartorial splendor. Nevertheless, I told myself, my client was vastly important, and therefore I was too. It didn't make me feel any better, but I didn't have time to figure out why.

Luckily, the folder Judi Kershay gave me contained everything, including a fax copy of the hotel confirmation sheet. I didn't even have to speak. I just handed it over, and the elegant personage was transformed before my eyes into a cooing sycophant.

"Hannah Couch is here!"

I took great pleasure in shushing her. "We don't want a scene in the lobby. Do you think you could just—"

"Of course. I'll show you up myself." She seized some plastic cards and passed them through a machine, then locked her drawer and came out from behind the polished marble countertop.

We went up in a special elevator that had to be operated with a key; the keys were those strips of plastic. I hoped there were enough keys for all of us. The woman from the desk cooed some more at Hannah, who accepted it graciously. Naomi watched, her expression dour.

The hotel suite was something else. It looked like the White House. A small foyer opened into a vast drawing room, full of antique tables and brocade-covered chairs and sofas, with lots of red silk draperies and priceless-looking oriental rugs on the floor.

Naomi nodded in approval. Kim, like me, was practically gaping with awe. Don was his usual laconic self, unimpressed by the splendor of a gilded ceiling inset with a Renaissance-style painting of frolicking cherubs and dripping with crystal chandeliers.

Hannah stood in the middle of the room, looking around critically. She went to the ornate fireplace surround and drew her finger across the mantel, then tested one of the gilt curlicues that supported the mantel. "Your maids don't dust," she said to our hotel escort.

"I'm sorry." The desk person, whose nameplate read JENNIFER, looked frightened. "I'll send someone up right away."

"Not now," Hannah said reprovingly. "Not while I'm in the suite. Do the dusting after I go out." She crossed to

25

the enormous arrangement of flowers that filled a crystal vase on the polished wood of a low central table. "These are lovely. Did you use preservative in the water?"

"Yes, I suppose so," Jennifer stammered. "Shall I check?"

"Don't bother. I'll know tomorrow." Hannah examined the rest of the room with pursed lips. "I hope my bathroom is clean. I don't like to see dirty corners anywhere, but especially not on a bathroom floor."

"Yes, Ms. Couch. I'll make a note of it." Jennifer began to look desperate.

"I believe in keeping up standards," Hannah said, bestowing a brief smile on the hapless woman.

Naomi headed for a set of the tall, carved doors that folded open on either side of the room. "Kim, Liza."

I jumped, but Kim was at the long windows that opened onto a balcony. "Look! The view!" She opened the windows, letting in a gust of cold, damp air, and went to hang off the balcony parapet. "What's that funny building over there? The Space Needle?"

Don joined her. "Isn't the Space Needle in Seattle?"

I joined them at the window. "That's the Transamerica Pyramid. Kind of ugly, but San Franciscans are used to it now."

"It's so cool." Kim smiled. Don snapped a picture of her against the San Francisco skyline.

"Excuse me." Naomi's voice was peremptory, summoning us back into the drawing room. "It's freezing out there. Please close the window."

"Sorry, Naomi." Kim darted back into the room, with Don following in a leisurely way that implied he was not to be ordered around.

Naomi sniffed. "Kim and Liza, check the kitchen and

26

get it set up with our utensils. Don, figure out where the best place to take a picture is, in case any of the interviewers insist. Hannah, you must rest for a few minutes."

Jennifer, the desk clerk, said in a trembling voice, "Oh, you had some messages. I should have brought them. I'll have them sent up. And may we say how honored we are that you chose to return to our hotel, Ms. Couch? Please, if you need anything else, anything at all—"

Naomi shook her hand briskly. "We'll be in touch."

I followed Kim into the kitchen, which was compact but well designed and very modern, with marble counters and glass-fronted cabinets. "Isn't the refrigerator kind of small?"

"I think that's actually the ice maker." Kim pulled out what looked like a deep drawer from the base cabinet. "These drawers are refrigerated. And the cupboards are pretty roomy." She started taking armloads of dishes and linens out of the big plastic footlockers and transferring them to shelves and cupboards. "Listen, I bet room service would send up milk and eggs and butter for the crepe batter." She giggled. "Especially if Jennifer spreads around what a dragon Hannah is. And I'll help you with the prep. The only problem is getting the shopping done. I don't know where they keep the food stores around here."

"I've got an idea about that." I stashed some copper pots and looked around for my knapsack. "I'll just make a few phone calls. Where's that cell phone Judi Kershay gave me?"

"Use the room phone. It goes on Hannah's bill, which goes on the publisher's bill, so you don't have to pay." Kim sounded worldly. I was impressed, but she added, "My mom told me to sign all my expenses on the room.

I'm not getting paid that much, and no tips. It makes sense."

"It does at that." I looked around for a phone.

"There's one by the sink. I think there might be one every five feet or so. I saw two in the living room, or whatever you call that room we were in—"

"The parlor?" Its grandeur had been rather intimidating. "The drawing room? The throne room?"

"I think that's some other room." Kim laughed.

I hurried into the drawing room to find my humble knapsack, with the list of phone numbers for the night's events. Only a couple of pieces were left from the tower of high-class luggage. My knapsack had been ignominiously discarded in the foyer.

Naomi appeared on the other side of the room and beckoned imperiously. "Come help Hannah unpack."

"I'm helping Kim with the kitchen," I began.

"You can get back to that." She pulled the last of the elegant suitcases toward the carved wooden doors. "Get that train case, would you?"

I slung my knapsack over my shoulder and bent to pick up the little leather bag. There was a knock at the front door. As I was in the foyer, I answered it.

One of those glittering bellhops, or whatever they were called in this exalted hostelry, stood outside, holding a silver tray heaped with envelopes. "Messages for Hannah Couch," he said, making a kind of half bow in my direction.

"Uh, thanks." I didn't know if I should scoop up the envelopes, or just take the tray. He solved the problem by coming into the room and sliding the messages onto another tray at a small gilt table beside the door.

"Is everything all right?" He glanced around the palatial space. "You're finding everything okay? Is Ms. Couch pleased with the suite?"

I wondered if he'd talked to Jennifer. "She should be," I said. "Yes, everything's fine."

Still he lingered, and I remembered that tipping was expected. Judi Kershay had given me petty cash for things like tips and bribes, which she explained were sometimes necessary. I pulled a bill off the wad she'd given me and passed it along to the bellhop. It disappeared into his palm.

"Oh, and by the way," I said, and he stood at attention. "We are desperately in need of really fast room service."

"The menu," he began, pointing toward the kitchen.

"No, not real food. I mean, not cooked food." The opulence was starting to get to me. "We need two gallons of whole milk, two pounds of butter, and a couple dozen eggs. Ms. Couch wishes to prepare crepe batter for a demonstration this evening."

"Of course," he said, nodding. "You want that as soon as possible?"

"Right." This time, I wasn't so slow peeling bills off the wad. He accepted them graciously, tipped his little organ-grinder's-monkey cap to me, and vanished.

I took the tray of messages in my free hand and, so burdened, followed Naomi. The carved doors led into a short hallway with two rooms opening off it. On the left was an opulent but empty bedroom, with luggage stacked near the bed. The door of the room on the right was shut. I took a deep breath and knocked briefly before going in.

Hannah lay on the huge, silk-covered bed, a black velvet eyeshade over her eyes. Naomi had evidently gotten over her mad. She bustled around, taking clothes from the suitcase and hanging them in the closet while she talked. ". . . don't know how that's going to work out." Her nasal whine would get on my nerves if she were my business partner. "And of course the schedule is all screwed up—" She broke off to glare at me. "You certainly took your time."

"Your messages arrived." I set down the train case and held out the tray full of white envelopes.

Hannah took off the eyeshade. She sat up, banking the pillows, and patted the bed beside her. "Here."

"You can read them while you're resting." There was something anticipatory in Naomi's voice.

"How the hell can I rest when you're yammering at me?" Hannah looked at the tray of messages fixedly for a moment, then at Naomi.

"Liza, Hannah needs a mineral water. Would you bring one?"

"It's Liz, actually." I knew the deliberate mispronouncing of my name was a way to keep me in line. I've always had trouble with lines. "Do you want lemon or anything?"

"You go with her, Naomi. Show her how to do it." Hannah's voice was commanding.

"But—" Naomi was still looking at the tray of letters.

"I am thirsty."

"Very well." Naomi flounced out of the room and I followed her, turning to close the door. Hannah was sorting through the envelopes; as I pulled the door to, she reached slowly to pick one out of the mass.

Following Naomi through the drawing room and into the kitchen, I wondered about the note Hannah had picked up. She hadn't opened it, but her expression as she regarded it was one of dread.

4

IN the kitchen, Kim turned from the last of the big crates and smiled at us. "Almost unpacked."

"Great." Naomi hardly looked at her. "Where's the Pellegrino?"

Kim took a big green bottle out of one of the cabinets.

"Hannah likes her water like this." Naomi filled a tall glass with ice. "Always a tall glass, never a short one. Always one slice of lime."

She gestured to Kim, who plucked a lime from a basket of citrus fruit on the counter and sliced it quickly.

"Squeeze the lime into the water," Naomi said in a lecturing voice, "then drop it in and stir." She suited action to word. "Got it?"

"I think I can do that." From the corner of my eye I caught Kim's grin, quickly suppressed.

"Fine. I'll take this to Hannah. Liza—"

"I'll give Kim a hand here and get the room set up for the interview." I felt lucky to have remembered this snippet from my lengthy list of instructions. "If that's okay, Ruth."

"Ruth? It's Naomi." She gave me a look of disgust.

"Oh, right. I'm sure I can remember that."

Naomi sailed from the room, and Kim collapsed in

nervous giggles. "You dare," she said. "She'll just get angry." She shivered. "She's really mean when she's angry."

"She's your aunt. You probably know."

"It's gotten worse the past couple of years. I think she's having that change of life thing." Kim piled the lime slices into a little container, popped on the lid, and put it in the refrigerator drawer. "She just lets herself be swept away with it, like she did in the limo."

"She seems over it now."

Kim shivered. "Yeah. It blows over, and she doesn't even remember the things she said. My mom says we have to make allowances, but it creeps me out."

"No kidding. Especially if she regularly goes around accusing people of murder."

"She didn't exactly—"

"She implied that Hannah caused her husband's death." I looked at Kim. "Do you know if that's possible?"

She looked uneasy. "I don't know. He died last year. I didn't really pay much attention, though I heard Naomi tell my mom it was something he ate. She said it in a meaning kind of way, you know?"

"Well, I doubt there's anything to it. And we have work to do." I dug the schedule out of my knapsack. As I'd hoped, the phone numbers of our destinations were there. "Listen, let me see if my idea about the food for the TV show works." I looked at the kitchen clock; twenty minutes until the interview, and we hadn't begun to be ready for the TV appearance. "If it does, can you carry the load until I see how the interview goes? I'm supposed to be sort of monitoring it and keeping it smooth."

"Poor you." Kim patted my arm. "I will be happy to prep the food. Much less hassle than what you'll be doing. It's just that there is a lot to do. I have to get all the ingredients prepped for both demonstrations, plus assemble a *huevos rancheros* casserole so it can cook while Hannah's showing how to make one. And I have to get that crepe batter made right away or it won't work."

"That should be under control. The bellhop will bring milk and eggs and butter."

I punched in the number of the contact person at Fanci-Foods Marketplace. "I'm calling on behalf of Hannah Couch," I said sweetly when he came on the line. "We're just checking to make sure everything is in order for this evening."

"Oh, yes. We've had a tremendous response, and are sure to have a standing-room-only crowd," he assured me.

"She'll be preparing *huevos rancheros*."

"Marvelous," he gushed. "That will be wonderful. What equipment should I collect?"

This was a stumper. I tried to think of the most indispensable piece of equipment Drake used in his gourmet forays. "We'll bring cookware and the like," I said, looking at Kim. She nodded encouragingly. "But there is something you could help us with. Of course, we want to prepare the dish ahead of time as much as possible, plus we're doing a cooking demonstration on *Live at Five*, and what with the interviews, I just don't have time to do the shopping. Could you all send over a few things? We'll be sure to give you and the event tonight a plug on *Live at Five*."

"Well, sure," he said. "What do you need?"

I ran down the list Hannah had rattled off in the limo, with Kim making a couple of whispered suggestions, and the man assured me he would personally pick out the produce and have our order delivered pronto. "As our thank-you gift to Hannah," he assured me. "In half an hour. No problem."

I hung up the phone and took a deep breath. "At least that went right."

"Good going." Kim looked at me in awe. "You said you'd never done this before?"

"Never before, never again," I muttered. "Okay, I have to call Judi Kershay and bring her up to date. Then I'll do the hostess thing in the drawing room. Is there anything I can do for you?"

"Nothing," Kim assured me. "Don's going to help me take all the bins but one down to the hotel's storage area after I get the crepe batter together, and then we might take a walk around the block. I don't need to be here until the market delivers our stuff, do I?"

"I wouldn't think so. Have a good time." I was already hauling out Judi Kershay's cell phone, programmed with her number. Just as it rang, a knock came on the front door. Kim darted off to answer it.

Judi answered on the first ring. "Liz! How's it going?" She sounded apprehensive.

"So far, so good." I gave her a rundown on what had been accomplished to date.

"Listen, you're doing a great job."

"I don't know." Kim came back from the front door, carrying a basket with all the crepe ingredients I'd asked room service for. She clattered around the kitchen, so I moved into the drawing room. I glanced over at the carved double doors that led into the rarefied bedrooms; they were closed, but I lowered my voice anyway. "Naomi hates me."

"She hates everyone," Judi assured me. "Don't worry about getting on her good side. I don't think she has one.

If you're tight with the food stylist, you're halfway there."

"She's very nice. And the photographer is nice too. He doesn't seem to mind being treated as a kind of *uber-busboy.*"

"And Hannah?" Judi sounded as if she'd braced herself. "How's she doing?"

"Okay. She seems fine." I hesitated. "Although there's something funny going on. She and Naomi are at each other's throats one minute, and then major pals the next minute. And Hannah seems—frightened of something. I don't know what."

"That doesn't sound like Hannah." Judi was dubious. "She's frightening, I grant you that."

"Maybe it's my imagination." I looked at the ornate grandfather clock in one corner of the room. "Listen, I have to set stuff up for the print interview."

"You sound like a pro already." Judi laughed. "You've really taken a load off my mind, Liz, I don't mind telling you."

"Wait until Friday before you congratulate me. I may end up bopping Naomi in the nose before this is over."

We hung up, and almost immediately I heard a knock on the front door.

The bellhop again. This time he carried a charming arrangement of forget-me-nots and ivy in a brass bowl.

"Oh, how pretty." I reached for the tip money again.

"My pleasure, ma'am." He smiled cheekily when he tipped his hat, and as he folded the bill, I saw I had given him a five instead of a one.

At least it wasn't my money. I set the flowers down and went through the checklist that Judi had given me for the room.

All ashtrays had to be removed. Smoking was banned from Hannah's presence, not because of health risks, but because it was bad for fabrics and ruined the palate for the delicate nuances of wines and foods.

I moved the magnificent bouquet from the low central table and put it on a table near the french windows; it was at least three feet across, and Hannah didn't like looking over flowers to see people. In its place I put the just-arrived bowl of ivy and forget-me-nots, which was less than a foot tall. The usual card-holder was missing from the arrangement; I checked back to make sure it hadn't dropped off in its brief journey from the door, and saw nothing.

Kim brought in a pitcher of ice water. "This is such a beautiful room. I wish I always lived in a place like this."

Naomi strode into the drawing room. "The telephone in my room isn't working." She plunked herself down in the library alcove and dialed up housekeeping to chew them out about that. Then she punched in another number, and began cooing into the phone. "How are my sweethearts? Mommy misses you. Mommy will bring you presents."

She went on like this for a few minutes. I raised my eyebrows at Kim, who drew me into the kitchen. As soon as the door was closed, she giggled.

"Her cats," she explained. "She has three, all spoiled. She calls and talks to them on the answering machine. She says they're happier that way."

Kim had washed some grapes from a complimentary fruit basket provided by the management and set them on the low table. No other food was allowed, because, according to Judi's notes, Hannah didn't want the interviewer to pay more attention to the food than to her.

The great woman herself came in just before the hour, to check out the room and give me instructions. She looked more like the glamorous grandmother of her book covers, made up and with her salt-and-pepper hair arranged in her signature bun, with loose waves framing her face. She wore a well-cut lavender suit and frilly white blouse, but looked as if she could whip on an apron and turn out a panful of cookies in no time.

"I will wait in my sitting room. You let him in"—she flicked her gaze up and down my thrift-shop-clad form—"and come to get me. I will sit on that sofa." She turned to gesture at the grouping of furniture around the low central table. "Make sure you seat him opposite, facing the window." She stopped abruptly, her eyes fixed on the bowl of ivy and forget-me-nots.

"Facing the window," I said helpfully, but Hannah wasn't listening. Her breath came in gasps; her face froze in a look of terror.

"What are those flowers doing there?" Her voice was a hoarse whisper.

"They just came, and since the arrangement was low instead of tall, I thought they'd do. I know you don't like tall flowers between you and the interviewer." I felt I was babbling, but the expression on her face was horrible. I looked around for help. No one else was in the room; I could hear Kim moving around in the kitchen next door, and from the other side of the suite, faint sounds from Naomi's room.

"Get rid of them." Hannah's face, under the carefully applied makeup, was ashen. "I'm going to go to my room now. Wait. Did a card come with the flowers?"

"No card. I thought that was odd."

37

"Odd is not the word," she whispered, and tottered off toward her room.

I carried the flowers into the kitchen. Kim stopped humming and looked askance when I pulled out the trash compactor and emptied the contents of the arrangement into it. "Why did you do that? Those were pretty."

"Hannah had a conniption when she saw them. Maybe she's allergic to ivy or something."

"Ivy? And little blue flowers?" Kim thought for a minute. "You know, someone gave her something like that at the airport before we left, and she just about jumped out of her skin. Must be an allergy." She looked wistfully at the flowers. "It would be nice to have people give you flowers all the time, don't you think?"

"As long as they don't say 'Drop dead' in the language of flowers." I put the brass bowl the flowers had come in aside. "There's the door."

I went to let in Randy Nevis from the *Chronicle*, wondering if Hannah would be up to seeing him. Wondering who would want to upset her like that, just before a media appearance.

5

THE food and entertainment editor, Randy Nevis, was tall and surprisingly slim for someone who spent a lot of time eating in restaurants. I guided him to his chair facing the window, but when Hannah made her entrance, he got up to greet her and then moved to a chair at right angles from her. This did not suit her, as I saw from her glare at me, but it was no part of hostessing to make the guest sit where he didn't want to, in my opinion. I offered drinks and retired to the kitchen to fix them. Hannah had asked for her signature Pellegrino with lime, and Mr. Nevis had seconded it.

I made two drinks in tall glasses, put them on a tray with an unopened bottle of mineral water, a bucket of ice, tongs, and a dish of lime slices. When I took the tray into the reception room, Mr. Nevis was talking politely to Hannah, who nodded and smiled sweetly. I set the tray of drinks down on the center table, next to the dish of grapes that replaced the arrangement of ivy and forget-me-nots.

Hannah offered Randy Nevis one of the glasses and took the other one, flashing me a steely glance after she looked at the tray. Obviously I'd done something wrong. Kim would have been able to put me straight, but she and

Don had gone out for a bit, and anyway, would the world come to an end if I put the tongs on the tray instead of in the ice bucket? At least, that was my guess for what was wrong.

Neither of them asked for anything else. Mr. Nevis got out a tape recorder and put it back when Hannah indicated that she didn't care for the infernal machines. Regal, composed, she looked capable of handling any trouble that came up. When the phone rang, I went into the kitchen to answer, leaving him to start the interview. As a freelance writer of magazine articles, I've done my share of interviews. I'd already decided what questions I'd ask if granted the privilege of talking to a celebrity like Hannah. I thought it would be amusing to hear how he went about it.

Jennifer from the front desk wanted me to know I had a delivery from FanciFoods. I asked if they could bring it up to the back door, assuming there was one, and she said yes. After I hung up, I went through the little hall at the back of the kitchenette to find the trade entrance to the suite.

Two ordinary-looking hotel rooms opened off the back hall. No brocade, no gilt, but the rooms looked comfortable, and each had its own bathroom. That made five bathrooms so far: one for each bedroom, and the powder room off the foyer. The suite was about four times larger than my little house in Palo Alto, where I had one of each room—bedroom, bath, living room, kitchen.

A door at the end of this hall opened into a service corridor, complete with freight elevator. This was the way the maids came. The elevator doors opened, and our personal bellhop appeared with a hand truck stacked with shopping bags and wooden crates. The Fanci-Foods people had done me proud.

The bellhop unloaded all the produce in the kitchen. I doled out more tip money, enjoying the lavish feeling of being generous with someone else's dough.

When I got back from seeing him out, Naomi stood in the kitchen doorway. "Don't make so much racket," she hissed. "Where's my glass?"

"In the cupboard, same as the rest of them." I waited a beat, then raised my eyebrows. "Shall I get you one?"

"Yes." She folded her arms and stood there, a tall woman much better suited to pulling down glasses from the cupboard than I am, since I'm only five-foot-two.

I focused on how much I was being paid and stretched to reach a glass. She wouldn't take it when I handed it to her.

"I want that one," she said, pointing back up to the shelf. "With ice and water and lime."

I set the glass down and looked at her. With her hair pulled back and that scowl on her face, she looked a lot like the Wicked Witch of the East. "Help yourself," I said, with a bit more emphasis than it needed. "I've got a bunch of stuff to prep here, so I'll just get on with it."

"You're making far too much noise," Naomi grumbled. She didn't move to get her own glass. "And you don't seem to understand your position. You are here to take care of our needs. If I need a glass, you get me one."

"Here's something for you to understand." I put both hands on my hips. "I'm here to facilitate Hannah's media contacts. If you want a personal maid, you can hire one."

"Sssh!" She looked over her shoulder and closed the kitchen door behind her to seal us into the little room.

41

"How dare you talk like that! I'm certainly going to let Judi Kershay know."

"You do that. And let her know that she'll have to find someone else for this job, because I don't put up with the kind of treatment you're trying to dish out. Maybe Judi will act as your personal servant."

This didn't sit well. "You can't do that. We have a contract!"

"Not with me, you don't. I have a contract with Judi. And nowhere in my contract does it say that I have to wait hand and foot on mean-spirited, able-bodied people. Get your own damned water and get out of my way, or I'm outta here."

Two red spots burned on Naomi's sallow cheeks. She seized the glass I had put on the counter and marched out, shutting the door behind her with an angry click.

When I turned around, Kim and Don were standing in the little hall that led to their rooms. Kim looked at me with mingled awe and dread.

"I've never heard anyone talk to Naomi like that. What did she do to get you so mad?"

"She was pushing me to see where I'd break. I have a low breaking point, that's all."

Don shook his head. "You've got an enemy there. A bad one."

"Yeah, well, there's nothing she can do to me. I'm a temp, not making a career out of this. And from what Judi Kershay says, Hannah and Naomi are definitely considered hardship cases around the media-escort scene. Naomi can complain about me all she wants, but everyone else will know whose fault it is really." I shrugged. "And if I get fired, big deal. Back to the temp pool."

Kim patted me on the shoulder. "You won't get fired right away. Naomi will want to have someone else in place before she boots you."

"Well, two can play that game." My dander was up. I don't expect royal treatment; I have worked hard for everything I have and in every job I take. But I also don't expect deliberate put-downs and snotty behavior. I had the dangerous thought that it might be time for someone to teach Naomi a lesson.

Kim looked at the crates and bags. "Is this the stuff from FanciFoods? I guess I'd better get busy."

"I'll help." I lifted a wooden flat of avocados. "They certainly sent enough."

"It's good to have a lot, because sometimes things get spoiled." Kim sorted through the grocery bags, putting things into order. "What great tortillas! We don't get them so fresh in Boston."

"The avocados are just right," I said, squeezing one gently. "Not too ripe."

"So here's the drill," Kim said briskly. "We don't cut up everything, because Hannah likes to show things before they're fussed with." She held up the knobby jicama and pretended to be Hannah. "You can easily find these at most markets. Peel off the skin to reveal the crunchy, sweet white flesh beneath." Her mimicry of Hannah's voice was surprisingly apt.

"You're good. You could do this." I took the jicama. "Shall I peel off the skin?"

"Yes, and cut it into batons—little sticks an inch and a half long and about half an inch wide. I'll check the crepe batter, then make the *salsa fresca*." She took out a tall plastic container of liquid from one of the refrigerator drawers and peered at the contents. "Setting up well."

She picked up a bunch of cilantro and went back to the last conversation but one. "At the restaurant, we have kind of contests to see who can sound the most like Hannah. Us counter people, I mean. And I won a lot. But I couldn't be on TV." She glanced over her shoulder. Don had melted from the room in the quiet, unobtrusive way he had. Kim confided, "I'm scared of the camera. One time this news magazine was interviewing us about working for Hannah Couch. They wanted me to say a soundbite thingy, but I couldn't do it with the camera on me."

She chopped tomatoes while I made jicama batons. We had to work shoulder to shoulder in the little kitchen, but we were getting it done. Kim was very fast with her knife; she had the salsa assembled before I'd finished my task.

"Put that jicama in this lemon-water," she instructed, splashing some water into a container and squeezing in half a lemon. "Then it won't discolor."

"You have to bring along all these containers and everything?"

"Yes, because when you transport prepped food, it has to stay nice."

"Did Hannah pack the equipment, or did you?"

"I did, mostly, though Naomi told me a few things not to forget."

"Well, you did a great job for someone who's never done it before."

Kim blushed. "I just tried to think of it as a massive catering job. I've done a bunch of those." She cleared away the cilantro stems and tomato seeds. "I'm going to get fruit ready for the compote now. You can cut up some more limes and lemons, and slice some avocados, and then we'll pack the cooler bags. When do we leave?"

I looked at the kitchen clock, wondering if I should get

44

a watch. "In about forty minutes. I'd better call and make sure the limo will be waiting. And then check on the interview before I slice anything."

The front desk assured me that they'd find the limo and make sure it was out front precisely at four. I hung up the phone and went into the drawing room.

The interview appeared to be going well. Hannah was laughing in ladylike tinkles.

"Really, Randy," she said to the interviewer. "How do you expect me to answer that? Of course I don't put myself on a level with Brillat-Savarin, or Escoffier. I am not trying to break ground in my work, simply saying that home cooks can hold their standards high and achieve more than they think."

Naomi had taken a seat near the interviewer. This plainly did not make Hannah happy; she kept shooting venomous looks at her partner. I checked the time again. Randy Nevis would have to go in twenty minutes, if Hannah was to have any time to change and rest before we left.

I felt a reluctant sense of admiration. Hannah might be a self-centered bitch, but what she did wasn't easy. This was only the second stop on her multicity tour. She would be at the media's beck and call until Friday, always having to chat and be nice to them, and then fly to another city and do it all over again. No wonder she liked to vent on the hired help. I felt a little sorry for her.

But not for Naomi. There were no media pressures on her. She could act like a human being if she wanted to. Now she was glancing at her watch every few minutes, keeping Randy Nevis aware that his time was running out. She didn't need to do that—it was my job. But I assumed she would keep at it, making it unnecessary for me to stay in the room.

I went back to the kitchen. Kim was slicing avocados, squeezing lime liberally over them as she worked.

"What can I do?"

"You can get those cooler bags out and set them up." She pointed her avocado-smeared knife at the pile of what looked like folded knapsacks. I picked one up and found that it was actually an insulated square container with a zip top and a handle. "I put the ice packs in that little freezer when we got here," Kim said, rubbing her cheek and leaving a smear of green behind. "They probably aren't frozen, but they're better than nothing."

"Shall I put them in now?"

"Better wait until just before we're ready to go." Kim slid the last sliced avocado into a container and sealed it. "I'm storing everything in the fridge for another half hour." She illustrated by putting the avocado into the refrigerator drawer, with the tidy stack of containers already there. "Good thing you got them to deliver the food. We'd never have been prepped in time otherwise."

"You have green on your cheek." I pulled off a paper towel and handed it to her.

"I'm going to go take a bath anyway." Kim waved a hand. "Soon as I clean up this mess."

"You go ahead. I'll clean this up, since I didn't do much of the prep."

She took me up on it, vanishing down the little hall to her room. I cleaned the counters and the sink, then peeked into the reception room to see how things were going there.

Randy Nevis was on his feet, thanking Hannah with what appeared to be sincerity for the opportunity to interview her. And she was all charm and goodness, thanking him for his patience and adding a motherly tip about his new baby. I went to act as doorperson and opened the door for him as Hannah ushered him to it, smiling graciously.

I shut the door behind him. Hannah turned, and all traces of graciousness vanished from her face.

"You're fired," she said to me in passing.

I blinked.

Hannah advanced on Naomi. "And you. Simpering and mewing and injecting yourself into my interview. Why do you think he was here, to interview the famous Naomi Matthews? What did you think you were doing?"

"I was trying to keep you on schedule," Naomi said shrilly. "Since she wasn't doing her job." She glared at me. "You said you wanted to rest before going to the TV station. You said you didn't want the interview to go past three-forty-five." She looked at her watch. "Well, I got him out of here just on time, and now you're having a temper tantrum. I won't put up with this, Hannah!"

"So don't put up with it. Run all the way back to Boston." Hannah's voice lost its usual quiet steeliness and began to climb toward shrill. "But don't think you can threaten me, Naomi. I know how to defend myself against that."

"You'd better hope your lawyer knows." Naomi's face was splotched with angry red. Her eyes were venomous slits. "I mean it, Hannah. If you don't listen to me, you'll be very, very sorry."

I didn't like to interrupt their hate fest. When I opened the foyer closet door to get my knapsack, both of them switched their glares to me.

"Where do you think you're going?" Hannah was the first to speak. Her voice could have cooled all the veggies Kim had prepped earlier.

"You fired me. I'm leaving."

"She's an insubordinate bitch." Naomi strode up to me. Before I saw it coming, she dealt me a stinging backhanded slap.

The room was silent. I rubbed my cheek, staring at Naomi, who stared back at me, her gray eyes blank. I looked at Hannah. She looked away.

"You slapped me." My voice shook. Naomi read that as a sign of fear. She smiled in slow satisfaction.

"Damned straight I did, and if you give me any more trouble—"

Her face, gloating in my discomfort, loomed over me. Her voice, that hectoring voice, set up strange vibrations in my head. Many years ago, I was married to a man whose hobby was beating me up. I had spent a long time trying to get out of that situation, and a longer time trying to figure out why I'd let myself stay in it. I was no longer a person it was safe to hit.

I slapped her in return. Her head rocked on her skinny neck. She backed away, tripped over a footstool, and sprawled on the floor.

Hannah made a high, strangled noise. I looked down at Naomi, who had her hand up to her face, her eyes wide in astonishment.

"Hitting is wrong," I said. "And one of the reasons why is because when you hit, people tend to hit you back. Nobody hits me, certainly not some tinpot food dictator. I'm making a full report of this incident to Judi Kershay. I don't expect anyone will be up for escorting you folks, once it's known you add physical abuse to verbal abuse."

I picked up my knapsack and turned to go. Hannah rushed up, right past Naomi, who was getting herself off the floor with no assistance from anyone else. "Wait. Where are you going?"

"You fired me." I tried to have patience, but I wanted to slap Hannah too. "And your associate hit me. In my book, that means I don't work here anymore."

"You can't just leave."

"Watch me."

She grabbed my arm when I would have opened the door. "No, I mean it. I didn't mean you were fired, just that you didn't do your job properly."

"You said fired. But if you'd rather, I'll quit."

"No, no. I want you to stay." She glanced at Naomi, who was anxiously scanning her face in the mirror. "Especially now. I like a woman who stands up for herself."

"I don't like a woman who stands by while her subordinates are battered."

Her eyes narrowed. "Perhaps we don't pay you well enough. Let me double your salary."

"It's not about money." I tried to find words of one syllable. "You can't treat people like this and keep them working for you. You're supposed to be so good at everything. Didn't you ever learn how to manage people?"

"Just stay through the next couple of days. Naomi won't bother you again. Will you, dear?" The question was acid-sweet. Naomi didn't bother to reply. If looks could have killed, Hannah and I would both be occupying slabs in the morgue.

"Judi would hate for you to leave. I would have to insist that my publisher no longer use her, and I could have her blackballed by everyone else, you know."

"You sure know how to sweet-talk a girl. Are your threats better than Naomi's slap?"

She sighed. "You're right, I know. I just feel a little desperate at being abandoned like this."

She looked desperate, to tell the truth. That's the reason why I stayed. Later, when I tried to explain it, no one believed me, but I truly felt sorry for the woman.

More fool I.

6

I called Judi Kershay from the television studio. We had scurried around to set up the mock kitchen with Hannah's pretty dishes. A carnival-glass bowl held raspberries for the *crêpes suzette* garnish, and an elaborate copper chafing dish was set up next to the disputed crepe maker. Kim had already used this to fix a quick dozen crepes with some of the batter she'd made earlier. Following her instructions, I'd poured whipping cream into the mixing bowl and sprinkled the raspberries with liqueur and sugar. She had set out a pitcher of orange juice and another pretty bowl, a little one, with orange zest.

Hannah was getting made up in her dressing room. I had checked before making my phone call. Naomi, despite her tight-lipped anger at Hannah and her venomous glares at me, hovered over the stylist in a proprietary way, telling him what shades of foundation to use and how to do the famous hair.

My face still stung from Naomi's slap, and my mark still reddened her cheek. Kim had cast speculative glances and evidently had pieced the story together, if her comforting pats on my shoulder were any indication.

I called from the only place that was relatively quiet,

51

the hallway outside the sound stage. Judi's office phone had rung unanswered, so I'd tried the second number.

"I don't understand. What happened?" Judi faded in and out intermittently. I deduced that she was in her car. It was nearly five o'clock, the time of going home from work. I wouldn't get home for hours.

"Hannah fired me. Naomi slapped me. I slapped her back. Hannah rehired me."

"Hold on. I'm pulling over." The static faded, and Judi's voice came through stronger. "Naomi hit you because Hannah fired you?"

"Not exactly." I told her how the whole thing went. "Could Hannah really take away your business like that?"

Judi's sigh came through loud and clear. "She could make things uncomfortable, but since no one wants to work with her, it might backfire."

"Well, I'm staying on the job for the time being."

"Bless you. Are you at the TV station?"

"Yes. Hannah's getting made up. Kim is a wonder; the prep is done for both events, and she's tuning up the crepe maker. I've checked with the FanciFoods contact, and we're all set there. In fact, they delivered the groceries to the hotel, which was a big help. If it wasn't for the people in charge, this would be a piece of cake."

Judi sighed again. "Well, hang in there if you can. But you're absolutely right. Nobody hits one of my employees. I'll have a word with the publicist."

"Would you find someone else to do this, before I totally alienate them?"

She hesitated. "That won't be easy. Can you stick it out just for tomorrow? After that, I might be able to take over. That would be punishment enough for Hannah."

"Why is she angry at you, anyway?"

"I promised I would never tell, and I keep my promises, so I can't tell you." Judi giggled. "You'd feel a lot better if I did, though. Suffice it to say that to a small extent, she's in my power. And I'll use that leverage. Just stay with it, Liz."

My turn to hesitate. "I can't make a firm commitment. If Naomi hauls off and hits me again, I'm gone. But I'll do my best."

"That's the most I can hope for." Judi sounded resigned. "Keep me posted."

I turned the phone off and stowed it in my knapsack. I slipped through the studio door, glancing at the enormous clock on the wall. The increase in frenzy of the people swarming around the stage would have told me it was nearly showtime, if the clock hadn't displayed the minutes ticking away until five. The audience area was only a hundred seats, and most were occupied. The kitchen set on the right side of the stage, empty now that Kim had finished her work, was unlit; intensely bright light was trained on the other side of the stage, where a desk with a few chairs made up the traditional talk-show milieu that had been around since the last time I owned a TV many years ago.

Kim came up and grabbed my arm. "You're supposed to be backstage before they start, because otherwise you'll have to stay out here, and then if something's needed there'll be trouble."

She hustled me along a twisting path through huge mechanical demons, stepping over piles of cables. "You seem to know a lot about it."

"I helped with a couple of TV appearances in Boston. People would go out front so they could watch; this one

53

girl who was Naomi's assistant wanted to be in the audience so she could try for a vacation cruise they were giving away as a prize. But when Naomi needed a copy of Hannah's new book—I believe that one was *Hannah Does Desserts*—the assistant was nowhere to be found. There was an incredible scene over it."

We scurried around the last big camera, just as theme music surged. "Welcome to Studio Three, where we're *Live at Five*," a disembodied voice said with increasing hysteria. The audience erupted into applause. Watching on the video monitor as a camera panned over the rows of people, I thought everything looked different; the studio looked bigger, the audience looked bigger.

The show's host bounced out, to more applause. Kim tugged me further into the recesses of the sound stage.

"Where's Don?" I had just realized that although Don had ridden to the studio with us, he had promptly vanished.

"He's set up over there." Kim pointed to the side of the stage where the kitchen was. The bright lights on the host's side made it hard to see into the shadows of the sound stage. I could vaguely discern a tripod, with a lanky form behind it. "He can't use a flash when he photographs her doing TV, so he has to have a tripod and special lenses to deal with it." She hugged her arms in excitement. "We can see the kitchen area from here."

I wasn't thrilled to listen to the host ask vapid questions of a series of guests, many of whom were excessively animated. My attention wandered to the audience members, and then farther afield, toward my house in Palo Alto, where Barker, my dog, would be pacing restively from the front door to the side door in the kitchen, waiting for me to come and take him for his evening sniff patrol.

Paul Drake would have to handle dog walking; he'd be home in half an hour, unless something came up at his work. He's a police detective with the Palo Alto Police Department. Our once-sleepy town is now considered a hot shopping and dining destination, and the crowds of people who throng University Avenue bring trouble in their wake, trouble that it's up to Drake and his fellow public servants to take care of. I hoped he would get off work in time to placate Barker. I wished I was there, laying a fire in my fireplace for evening warmth, going over to Drake's kitchen to see what he was cooking for dinner.

Kim poked me. "Hannah's up."

From our vantage point we could see her thread her way behind the scenes until she reached the kitchen set. She stepped behind the counter, and the lights above her blazed.

She was a pro, I had to admit. Transformed from the dowdy, nondescript woman she was without makeup, she smiled her motherly smile and took the audience into her confidence about how to zest an orange, how to make the crepe batter, how to use her newest device, the crepe maker which her staff had developed following her instructions. That was what she said, anyway. I didn't dare look around to see how Naomi took that. In fact, I was surprised she didn't storm the stage. Hannah plugged the evening's appearance at FanciFoods.

By the time Hannah was through, I thought how easy *crêpes suzette* was and how I should cook it for Drake sometime.

"Damn, she's good." Kim was grinning. "She leads them along, but doesn't talk down to them."

"Yeah. Why can't she be like that in life?"

Kim shrugged. "Typical celebrity behavior. Once a big movie star came into the shop. She was doing some event in Boston. She wanted us to cater a big party she'd decided to have that very night. We told her what we could do at such short notice, but that wasn't good enough. She had to have all this complicated food. We said no thanks, and she pitched such a hissy fit you wouldn't believe. Screaming, literally. And then she stomped out, and this woman in the street stopped her to tell her what a fan she was, and we saw her oozing gracious charm. They just have different buttons than real people, that's all."

The host escorted Hannah to his desk, showing the copy of *Hannah Hosts Brunch* that I had placed there earlier. She smiled and nodded, answering questions, laughing at his jokes, and served him some of the raspberry-sprinkled crepes with their aromatic liqueur-laced sauce. She was far more at her ease in front of a camera than I could ever be.

The audience enjoyed it too. They were smiling, laughing, hanging on Hannah's every word. After my gaze circled the auditorium, I saw Naomi standing a few feet from us. She, at least, was not impressed. Her face wore a malevolent scowl as she watched Hannah perform.

"Don's packing up," Kim said, nudging me. In the shadows behind the now-darkened kitchen set, we saw Don fold his tripod and stuff cameras into a bag. "We'd better do the same."

She slipped around to the kitchen set, and I followed, wondering what we could do when the show was still going on. Swiftly, noiselessly, Kim packed all the dishes in the carriers, sliding the leftover food onto a disposable tray she'd brought along. I tried to help, but she was much quieter than I was.

The host announced a commercial break, and Kim started hustling her crates and cooler bags onto a hand truck. Don came over to help us. The stagehands just watched. "Union," Kim hissed when I complained. "They have very strict rules."

We called the limo around and got everything put away, then went back up to wait for Hannah to be through. She was still on the show, relegated to a farther chair, chatting a bit with a glossy-looking young woman whose picture I'd seen in some checkout line somewhere. The young woman confided artlessly that she planned to marry soon, and what would Hannah suggest to serve at the wedding?

My attention wandered again. I needed to keep track of the time to make sure we got to the FanciFoods demonstration by six-thirty, to allow time for setup. It worried me. If Hannah chose to stick around talking on TV, I didn't know how I was going to stop her. Go on camera and drag her off? Not acceptable. I decided to leave that particular worry to Naomi, who probably had ways of dealing with any such problems.

Naomi wasn't standing at the side where she had been. She wasn't anywhere in the audience that I could see. Troubled, I poked Kim, who stared entranced at the glossy young man who'd replaced the glossy young woman at the host's side.

"Where's Naomi? How do we spring Hannah?"

"Relax," Kim whispered back. "Hannah knows what time it is. We don't have to leave until six, you said."

"That's if traffic is not too bad." The FanciFoods store in Pacific Heights was halfway across San Francisco. If traffic was gridlocked, it could take closer to an hour to get there, and Hannah's class/demonstration began at seven-thirty. "Where's Naomi, anyway?"

"She probably went to Hannah's dressing room to get everything ready. Hannah won't wear that TV makeup for an instant longer than she has to. They really glop that stuff on. But she'll be quick getting it off, and then we'll go. You'll see, Liz."

I worried for nothing. In a few more minutes, another commercial break came along, and this time, in the game of talk-show musical chairs, Hannah was out. She thanked the host and was ushered off the stage. Kim led the way to a corridor with dressing rooms opening off it. "Let's just wait here," she suggested. "Those rooms are tiny, and there's nothing to see anyway."

There was nothing to see, but plenty to hear. "Can't get away with it," Naomi shouted shrilly. "My attorney—"

Hannah's words were harder to discern. "Signed the agreement—"

Naomi cut in. She was practically gibbering, but as far as I could tell, she'd moved the argument away from the crepe maker. "Morton . . . investigation," we heard. Kim and I looked at each other, raising our eyebrows.

Hannah's answer came in a lull in the incessant noise of the stagehands. "If it's investigations we're talking about, what about your brother Tony's death? That was convenient for you, wasn't it, dear?"

Naomi was silent for a moment. I looked at Kim. Her face was white. "What's she talking about?" she whispered to me. "My uncle had a heart attack. We always joked about him using so much butter and cream. No one was really surprised."

I strained to hear Naomi's reply, but for once she wasn't

shouting; all that came through the door was a low rumble. The doorknob turned.

"Let's get back a little," I hissed, and we stepped quickly away. I was acting on instinct; something told me that if they knew we'd overheard their conversation, things would be even more unpleasant.

Hannah swept out of the dressing room, followed by Naomi with a more than usually sour expression on her face.

"Let's go," Hannah said brusquely. "Where's my water?"

She looked at me, but I hadn't thought to provide myself with water.

"It's in the limo." Kim threw herself into the breach.

"Let's move then. We can't hang around here anymore."

We followed her into the elevator and out to the car. No one spoke. Hannah scowled. Naomi sulked.

Don brought up the rear with Kim, but his teasing didn't make her giggle as it usually did. When we got to the limo I would have to paw through the cooler bags to find the bottled water. "Did we bring a glass?"

She looked at me blankly, then seemed to hear what I said. "I sure didn't. She'll have to swig from the bottle like everyone else does."

"Kim—about what she said—about your uncle—"

"I can't talk about that now. I can't even think about it." Kim pressed her hand to her throat, as if to hold her head on. "I'm sure it was just a lie. My aunt might be hard to get along with, but she's not—she wouldn't—"

Hannah reached the limo; the driver opened the passenger door at her regal nod. Kim turned away.

Hannah slid onto the seat, then stopped.

I peered over her shoulder into the limo to see what the

hang-up was. She stared fixedly at the square white envelope that rested on the leather seat.

"Someone left you a fan letter, looks like." I thought that would make her happier and relieve some of the tension she exuded.

I was wrong. She looked at the envelope as though it was a snake. Finally she reached to pick it up. She looked at Naomi, who had gotten in the other door. Naomi looked back, her eyebrows raised in a silent question. Don resumed his seat by the chauffeur, and Kim and I crawled into our seats facing backward. But those two didn't even notice me scrounging through the bags. They were busy staring at each other.

Finally Hannah turned away, tucking the note into her handbag. I noticed she used only her fingertips, as if she was saving the fingerprints. Naomi noticed too.

"Aren't you going to read it?"

"No." Hannah didn't look at Naomi. She stared straight ahead, not looking at Kim or me either. "I have an idea what it says. I'll just save it for the lab."

"Lab?" Naomi's voice came out as a croak. "What do you mean, lab?"

"I hear they can find DNA these days in even the smallest amount of saliva. Whoever licked that envelope to seal it left their DNA. The police will be able to find out who's—" She broke off, noticing Kim and me. I was frankly hanging on every word.

"Since when do you take your fan mail to the police?" Naomi scoffed, but her voice sounded nervous.

"I think you can pinpoint it, if you try." Hannah looked at Kim. "You said my water was out here."

"Here." Kim handed over the green glass bottle I had placed in a cup holder. "I didn't bring a glass. Sorry."

Hannah took the bottle, but reluctantly. "You know how I like it." She looked at me. "You should know too."

"Ice halfway up the glass, water, a lime wedge squeezed and then dropped into the glass." I spoke promptly. "Kind of hard to produce in a car, though."

Hannah leaned forward and pressed a button on what I'd thought was just a console between Kim's and my seats. A door swung open, revealing a small refrigerator compartment, which contained tiny bottles of liquor and wine, but no glasses or lime.

"There are ways," Hannah said, "of doing almost anything, if you're motivated enough." She stared at Naomi as she spoke, and her voice was very cold.

We rode the rest of the way in silence.

7_____

JUDI Kershay walked into the demonstration area of the FanciFoods store at 7:10. I was so glad to see her I almost cried.

"Thank God you're here. Everything is too, too weird."

She patted me on the shoulder. "Let's make sure the event is set up right, then we'll talk."

Kim and I had been very impressed with the demo area when we'd arrived twenty minutes earlier. The store was a lush temple to food, with sparkling black and white floor tiles and lavish displays of everything edible, not to mention a gourmet take-out section that Kim said rivaled the place where she worked in Boston. On the second floor, up a winding staircase that gave panoramic views of reverent produce pyramids, was an auditorium of food with raked seating. Even those in the back could easily see the action on the gleaming marble counter, inset with stove burners and backed with a rank of ovens, the whole area reflected in a huge, tilted overhead mirror that projected the action to the audience.

Kim had started right in assembling the spare casserole of *huevos rancheros*; she was sprinkling its top with grated *queso fresco*, which Greg, the FanciFoods event coordinator, had been only too happy to supply. The air was scented with chorizo and the tortillas she'd heated on the *comal* that had been part of Hannah's equipment. I had been the scullery maid, cleaning up her pots and pans while she worked swiftly to assemble the layers of tortillas, chorizo, and the salsa-like tomato sauce. She had poached eggs in the wide skillet without any trouble at all. Watching Drake poach eggs, I had gotten the idea that it was a major operation with a chancy outcome, but Kim did it in minutes with no fuss. She'd nestled the eggs into hollows in the sauce that topped the warmed tortillas and chorizo, before sprinkling on the grated cheese. She put the casserole in the oven, and Greg showed us how to program it to bake the dish and then turn off.

I introduced Judi to Kim. "What do you want us to do?"

"I'm just going to cut up some more limes and make sure all the condiments are okay." She had arranged a pottery bowl of avocados, limes, and peppers on the counter. "Liz, could you look in the cooler and find that container of sliced avocado? And the jicama batons you cut this afternoon?"

I checked in the zippered cooler bags, bringing out the containers she wanted. "Here. Should I put them on a plate or something?"

"These bowls look nicer." Kim handed Judi a couple of terra-cotta-colored bowls with Aztec motifs, shinily glazed. "Could you do that? And Liz, find the paprika in the crate under here and put some in this little dish." She handed me another terra-cotta dish, this one very small, stamped with a pattern of blackberries and twining vines. I filled it with paprika while Kim squeezed a couple of limes into its twin.

"What's this for?"

"The jicama. You dip the end in lime juice, then in paprika. It makes a nice-looking accompaniment."

"I did these," I bragged to Judi, showing her the tray of drink skewers I'd made with alternating maraschino cherries and small cubes of prickly pear cactus. "For the tequila sunrises."

"The Sunrise Brunch Beverage," Kim corrected absently. She'd set up one end of the counter with a pitcher of orange juice, another of grenadine, a bottle of tequila, and the skewers. "You can make them without booze."

Judi admired the skewers, then looked around. "Where's Hannah? For that matter, where's Naomi?"

Kim cast a worried glance behind the demonstration area, where a hallway led to offices and restrooms. "Hannah's freshening up in the manager's private bathroom. Naomi was supposed to help her, but when I was back there, she'd found the manager's private stock of Scotch."

"Naomi's drinking?" Judi pursed her lips.

"She isn't an alcoholic or anything," Kim said defensively, "but when she starts, it can get ugly."

"Thanks for the tip." I couldn't figure out how Naomi could get any meaner, and wasn't anxious to know firsthand.

"Fill me in quickly," Judi said as we left Kim at the counter, mincing scallions. "And aren't you lucky," she added, "that the food stylist is very nice and willing to do the prep work. Usually they are picky about what they do."

"Kim's delightful." People were coming up the stairs for the event. Platters of fruit and cheese and bottles of red and white wine had been set out on a side counter, and the customers stood around convivially, chatting as if it was a party. "It's very nice here. Must be costing FanciFoods an arm and a leg to put all this food out."

"The audience paid handsomely to attend." Judi nodded at a couple of women nearby, each of whom clutched a copy of *Hannah Hosts Brunch*. "This is the first program in a series. FanciFoods was lucky to get such a big name to kick it off."

Naomi appeared at the hallway opening. She pushed her way through the crowd around the food and helped herself recklessly to the sauvignon blanc.

Judi watched this with a brooding eye. "So what's happening? Put me in the picture."

"Naomi and Hannah have been fighting practically since the moment they landed. It got really nasty in the dressing room at the TV station."

"They were yelling?" Judi grimaced. "Terrible place to pick for a falling out. There'll be gossip for sure."

"It seemed kind of personal. Each of them accusing the other of—well, eliminating anyone who stood in the way. It was not pleasant." I hesitated. I have had some experience, not of my choosing, with people driven to the extreme of murder. The vibes I felt around Naomi and Hannah were horridly reminiscent of that. "Do you think they would really do anything? Like hurt each other?"

Judi made tut-tutting noises, but she looked worried. "I don't think it would come to that. You say they accused each other of that—of murder?"

The word hung between us.

"Not really." I shivered a little. "But there was a nasty scene earlier when Naomi found out Hannah was going to promote the new crepe maker on TV. Naomi claims to have invented it, but Hannah sure didn't give her any credit."

"I caught the show." Judi stared at Naomi, gulping the wine as if it was Kool-Aid. "Hannah is very good at what she does."

"Good at the performance aspect, and at knowing everything about food. She's not good at people."

"That has never been a requirement for being a celebrity," Judi said. "A lot of them aren't good at people." She took a deep breath. "Let's go beard the lioness and see how bad it is."

I held her back. "Judi, I hope I haven't ruined your business. If I'd known what I was doing—"

"You didn't ruin anything." She gave me a reassuring smile. "Even a pro would have been hard-pressed to respond differently when slapped. Don't worry about it. I sure won't. There are other fish in the sea besides Hannah Couch, and some of them are not only nice to work with but glad to be my clients. I'll survive."

I followed her down the hall into the manager's office. Hannah was just emerging from the manager's bathroom. She had fixed her hair without Naomi's assistance, and it showed by being a bit less perfect than usual. Her makeup had been skillfully applied, though. She looked formidable, an iron-haired woman at the peak of her powers.

"Well, Hannah." Judi stopped in the door to the manager's office. "I just stopped in to monitor the tour. How are you doing?"

Hannah scowled at both of us. "I would be doing better if you'd given me a professional instead of this ignorant woman." Her indignation lent a spark to her stern countenance. "She knows absolutely nothing about keeping the clients happy."

"Is it necessary for the clients' happiness to beat on the

escort?" Judi sounded mild, but I could tell she was upset. "Because that isn't allowed. If you want to physically abuse your help, you had better go elsewhere to find it."

The two locked glances, and Hannah looked away first. "It wasn't me," she mumbled. "It was Naomi. I don't condone that sort of behavior. I've spoken to her. And I gave the girl back her job."

I didn't know whether to be flattered at being called a girl—something that has not happened to me since I turned twenty, and that was fifteen years ago—or irritated at the idea that I was so unimportant that my name could be forgotten at will.

"It's not for you to give or take away," Judi said gently. "You signed a contract with my agency. I do all the staffing. Frankly, no one on my staff wants to work with you. If I cut you loose, and word of this slapping gets around, you will be hard-pressed to find any reputable public relations firm to deal with."

"I can do it myself if I have to," Hannah said, tossing her head. "I did when I started out."

"Right. You call up Leno's people and tell them you want to be on the show." Judi snorted. "You don't have the Rolodex for it anymore, dear." She gave Hannah that measuring look again. "I told Liz I'd take over the rest of your stay here."

"You?" Hannah appeared to be trying to find words. "No. No way. I certainly don't want you around."

"That makes it mutual, as I don't want to be around." They stared each other down again, and again Judi won. "But if you can't keep a lid on it and be pleasant, and make Naomi be pleasant, that's what you'll get. Me."

"This is, quite simply, blackmail." Hannah narrowed her eyes. "You didn't tell her—"

"I've said nothing to anyone, as per our agreement." Judi was adamant. "But if no one else will work with you, and no other agency in town will touch you, you'll be stuck with me. This time only. Next time, I won't be able to help you out at the last minute. Your reputation as a horrible person to work for is going to make it difficult for you when *Hannah Cooks for the New Millennium* comes out."

"How did you—" Hannah pressed her hands to her face. "Listen, I have a demonstration to do. You're purposely upsetting me before I have to go out and appear in front of an audience. And I might add that this is my third public appearance today. I would think you, of all people, would have some sympathy. I am not feeling well."

Judi studied her thoughtfully. "You'll do a wonderful job. You always do. And it's very simple, really. I only want reassurance that you will treat my employees with the utmost respect while they're working with you. It wouldn't hurt you to treat all your employees the same way, but that's not my concern."

"Okay, okay." Hannah smoothed her hair. "I'll speak to Naomi. Not that she'll listen," she added, low-voiced. "She's drinking, and that's always a bad sign. But I'll do my best to make Liz here feel happy." She gave me a saccharine smile. "Is that good enough to avoid your tender ministrations?"

"For the time being." Judi stepped aside from the doorway, just as Naomi came lurching down the hall.

"Where's our little star?" Naomi said loudly. "Where's that celebrity chef? Where's little Hannah got to? Her audience is waiting." She dragged out the last word.

Hannah looked exasperated. "Naomi, how could you start drinking? You promised . . ."

"Promises, promises." Naomi was singing, though it took a minute for that to become apparent. "Promises are nothing," she said with emphasis, coming right up to Hannah, who recoiled from the wine breath. "A dime a dozen."

"If you're going to start this, you'll have to go home." Hannah stepped around Naomi to get to the doorway. "You know we talked about this."

"You talked, as usual." Naomi began to look sullen. "You talk way too much, know that? But you don't say what the people want to hear."

"And you know what the people want to hear?" The casual contempt in Hannah's voice was somehow shocking.

"They want to hear this! 'Naomi Matthews invented this wonderful crepe maker.' Not you! That was mine! You stole it, you bitch!"

Swaying, Naomi started for Hannah, her slapping hand raised. But Hannah was quicker off the mark than I was. She pushed Naomi farther into the office, then joined us in the hallway, shutting the door in Naomi's face and producing the key from her pocket. Dimly we could hear Naomi cursing, but it was a well-constructed door.

"She can sleep it off until we leave," Hannah said, putting the key back in her pocket. "She'll quiet down once she sobers up a bit."

I exchanged glances with Judi. Perhaps Hannah didn't realize that most doors could be unlocked from the inside.

Perhaps Naomi didn't realize it either. She banged on the door and hollered a little bit, then was silent.

Judi and I trailed down the hall after Hannah. She strode ahead, ignoring us, and swept out into the demonstration room to great applause. The clock on the wall said 7:27. Two more hours until the end of a long and exhausting day, for all of us.

"You don't need to stick around if you don't want to," Judi said. "I'll tuck them into the limo for the trip back to the hotel. Why don't you get the driver to take you home? He can get to Palo Alto and back here before nine, and we won't be ready to leave until after then."

"That's very tempting." My little house, my refuge, had never been more desirable.

"But can you come to the City early tomorrow? It's another long day. That radio interview at seven, and then the Cordon Bleu in Sonoma County at ten, and a bookstore in Santa Rosa at one P.M., then Berkeley at seven P.M. Lots of riding in the car."

I must have cringed, because she searched my face with concern. "Would you just as soon not do any more?"

I thought of that lovely money. With the money Judi was giving me for these four days, I could easily pay my property tax and have a bit left over for the emergency fund. Then I could write next week instead of looking for more temp work.

"I'll do it. The worst is probably over." Even as I said the words, I knew it was a lie. Driving around the Bay Area with Hannah and Naomi, no matter how luxurious the automobile, was going to be awful. But a lot of temp work is awful, and not nearly so well paid.

"Great." Judi looked relieved. "Get along, now. Just be there tomorrow before seven A.M. so you can facilitate the radio interview, then herd them around to the other events."

The limo was waiting when I stepped out of the Fanci-Foods store. Judi had called the driver, and he opened the back door with a flourish. I had it all to myself for the forty-five-minute ride to Palo Alto, and I reveled in every minute. I opened the refrigerator, though I didn't drink anything for fear that Hannah had counted all the little bottles of wine and booze. I found controls for music, air, even humidity, and played with them all.

The driver let me off in front of Paul Drake's house. Both houses on the long lot had come to me, but Paul was buying the house in front; I kept the little cottage in back. My half of the lot was roomy enough for a good-sized garden as well as running space for Barker.

I could hear Barker; Drake had let him out, and he was charging up and down the fence that separated my house from Drake's parking area. I went to quiet him.

He was happy to see me, but no happier than I was to be home. While I petted him and smoothed his black and white fur and kept him from planting his big paws on my shoulders, Drake's kitchen door opened.

"So you're back." He stood in the doorway, rumpled, his wiry hair standing out around his face, holding his place in a book with one finger. "How was your day as a worker bee?"

"You wouldn't believe the half of it."

He shivered. "Don't stand out in the cold. Bring your dog and tell me about it. I saved you some dinner."

I opened the gate for Barker, and we hustled into the golden light of Drake's warm kitchen.

8

I drove into San Francisco early the next morning with the commuters, instead of taking the train. The train has many advantages, but in case there was more shopping to do, I wanted some transportation. My '69 VW bus, called Babe because it was blue and somewhat oxlike in disposition, was actually a great commute car that traveled well at thirty to forty miles an hour. I didn't have much occasion during my drive to reach its top speed of sixty.

The sky was still dark when I got to the city. I made my way to Nob Hill, dodging delivery trucks, bike messengers, and homeless people. The entrance to the hotel's parking garage was guarded by a gnome who peered suspiciously at me and my clunky transportation.

"Are you a guest? This garage is for guests only."

"I'm working for one of your guests. Hannah Couch." I didn't remember the room number. "One of the big suites. Possibly the Presidential one."

He turned away to speak into a telephone, then let me in, directing me to a parking place far to the back, I guess so the bus was less visible amongst the Mercedes and Jaguars and even Rolls-Royces I saw as I drove to my corner. On the way to the elevator, I stopped to tell him, "It's a classic, you know. Extremely valuable. Don't let anyone steal it." Judging from his blank stare, he didn't believe me.

The elevator was quiet and luxurious. Because it was chilly outside, I'd worn jeans and a sweater; there didn't seem to be much point in dressing up to please Hannah, when she was not capable of being pleased.

I got out at the lobby to take the elevator to the Presidential Suite and discovered that it required insertion of a room key before it would take me there. I didn't have a key. I could have asked the front desk clerk to take me up, but it grated on me to have to supplicate like that. I saw a bellhop with a cart piled with luggage, and by following him I found the freight elevator. He didn't say anything when I got on. I got off at my floor and knocked at the kitchen door.

Kim opened it. "There you are. I wondered when you'd get here." Her eyes were big in her thin face. She hustled me into the kitchen and closed the door.

"They've been at it all night," she whispered. "I don't know how much more I can take. Naomi went through every one of the little bottles of booze in the limo, and then she drank a bunch of stuff from the bar here. She was yelling, and Hannah yelled back. It's been impossible. They didn't knock off till way after three this morning."

Don came into the kitchen. "You should have come out with me. Not stay here and listen to those two old biddies claw at each other."

Kim didn't smile. "I felt someone should be here. Just in case . . ."

"In case one of them jumped the other one?" Don smiled derisively. "Not likely. They're just having a cat fight."

73

"I don't know." Kim hugged herself, shivering despite the thick sweater she wore. "After what Hannah said, I just don't know. I kept thinking about my uncle. His death was kind of sudden. What if Naomi did cause it? What else would she do?"

We stood around the kitchen in uneasy silence for a moment. "Hey, kid," Don said finally. "Don't go looking for trouble."

"I couldn't stop thinking about it. And they wouldn't stop going at each other." Kim dug a tissue out of her pocket and blew her nose. "It was awful."

I set down my knapsack on the table and searched for a way to turn the conversation away from Kim's fears about her aunt. "They'll be ready to make up today."

"Either that or Hannah will send Naomi off." Don patted Kim awkwardly on the shoulder. "You'll see. I'm going to get my cameras ready."

He vanished into his room.

"Hannah told me she wanted to prepare crepes again," Kim said dolefully. "But I think that was just to make Naomi mad. Can we cook at the bookstores?"

"Let me check the schedule." I opened the knapsack and shuffled through papers. "It says here we're supposed to give out cinnamon roll-ups. Whatever they are."

"I made them." Kim pointed to a neat stack of white boxes on the table. "We brought along a stock of Hannah's special boxes, and since I couldn't sleep last night, I baked. But this morning she came out and said we were going to do crepes."

"She is wrong." I sniffed. The air did indeed have the scent of cinnamon.

"Well, don't tell her that." Kim looked apprehensive. "She's so stubborn, you know."

The woman herself swept into the room. "Finally you're here." She didn't look as if she'd spent most of the night arguing; her hair was arranged in its rigid iron curls, and her makeup was perfectly applied. "You're late. We do have a schedule to keep, you know."

"The radio interview is in fifteen minutes." I went past her into the main room. "Where do you want to be during it? On this sofa? Is Naomi going to be out here?"

Hannah looked down her nose. "She doesn't need to be present. She doesn't need to come with us at all today. Perhaps she'd rather stay and find a bar."

"I'll check that the limo will be ready by seven-forty-five." I escaped to the kitchen, and Kim followed.

Unfortunately, Hannah followed Kim. "I want some water. That room-service coffee was terrible. And they didn't snip the end of the rose before putting in the vase; it's already starting to droop."

Kim pulled out the familiar green bottle. Silently she got ice and a lime wedge.

"Make me one too." Naomi pushed in at the kitchen door. The little room was crowded, and not just with people; the bad vibes were rife. "My throat is as dry as Hannah's shortbread."

Hannah didn't rise to the bait. She took her glass of water and stalked into the living room.

Naomi wouldn't let up, though. She grabbed her own glass before Kim had even finished pouring it, and followed Hannah out the door. Plunking down her glass right next to Hannah's on the polished mahogany coffee table, she slumped into a chair. She didn't look perky at all. Her hair was pulled back in its usual severe bun, but wisps escaped to straggle around her sallow face, and the lines around her mouth seemed deeper than usual. Her hand shook when she reached for her glass.

"That's my glass." Hannah spoke sharply. Naomi didn't acknowledge the words, but she did change the direction of her grasping hand. Her grip on the glass wasn't good; its ice-beaded sides slipped through her fingers and landed on the oriental rug, spilling all over Hannah's elegant Italian pumps.

"God damn it." Hannah leaped to her feet. "You idiot. You drunken, washed-up has-been."

"No more yelling." Naomi put a hand to her head. "You did enough of that last night. People might get the perfectly correct idea that you're a shrewish bitch." She looked down at the mess on the carpet. "But I'm sorry about the shoes. They were very nice."

Hannah kicked off the shoes and upended one. More water dripped onto the carpet. "Now I'll have to change."

"Can't you wait until after the interview?" I looked at the clock. The radio station would be calling in ten more minutes.

"I don't like having wet feet. Stall them if they call before I get back." Hannah stalked off toward her bedroom, and I ran to the kitchen for a cloth to sop up the mess, then returned to the living room. Kim came out to help me, while Naomi staggered into the kitchen and returned in a minute with another glass of water.

Kim picked up ice cubes and dropped them into the glass Naomi had overturned. "This beautiful rug," she said in distress.

"Bitch deserved it." Naomi put her new glass carefully on the table next to Hannah's, and shook her finger at

Kim. "Don't bother to defend her. Look how she's treating your poor old aunt."

Kim flushed. "Aunt Naomi—"

"She's a snake. 'Oh, Naomi, what a clever crepe maker. Of course I'll be glad to produce it for you. Sign here.' What an idiot I was. But she'll pay."

"Don't talk so crazy." Kim looked nervously down the hallway. "She'll be out soon for her radio interview, and then we'll have to load up and go."

"Not me." Naomi's expression of concentrated malevolence was frightening. "I'm never going to hop to her command again."

"Naomi—"

"Don't you Naomi me." Naomi drew herself up. "Do you want to always be some little jumped-up gofer? You're a fool, Kim. You want to see what happens to Hannah's help? Just take a look. I know you think you could do my job. But I'm not going quietly. No one pushes Naomi Matthews around and gets away with it. You hear me?"

Hannah strode back out into the room, once more perfectly groomed. "The whole damned hotel can hear you." She looked down at Naomi with contempt.

"Let them hear me. As long as everyone knows you for the bitch you are, I don't care."

Kim, looking distressed, pushed one of the water glasses over to her aunt, but Naomi didn't notice, so concentrated was she on Hannah.

"Since your livelihood is bound up in my career, I'd think you would care." Hannah bent over, picked up a glass of water, and took a long swallow.

Naomi smirked. "You might be surprised."

"What? You're going to quit?" Hannah looked down her nose. "I don't think so."

"You don't think at all. If you did, you wouldn't tangle with Naomi Matthews." Naomi raised her own glass, sloshing some of the water onto the floor. "To you, Ms. Hannah Goddamned Couch. Or should I say 'Roxy Ripper, Sexy Stripper'?"

Hannah stilled. "Don't go on with that, Naomi. It wouldn't be healthy for you."

"You'll find out who it's not healthy for." Naomi drank some of her water, watching Hannah intently. "Yes, I'm enjoying writing my book. Did you like the first couple of installments, Hannah? I have some tales to tell. And I will tell them. You bet I will."

"You have nothing to say that anyone would be interested in." Hannah set her glass down with a thunk.

"You seemed interested." Naomi's voice held a cold taunt.

"So it was you. I thought so." Hannah took a step forward. Her hands clenched. "To think I trusted you." She breathed deeply, her nostrils flaring. "You better not have shown that to anyone else."

"I haven't yet. But I think I will." Naomi drained her glass, and reached out to set it on the table. She missed; the glass fell onto the carpet, making another wet spot. Kim knelt to apply the cloth once more.

"Naomi, you're still drunk." Hannah sounded disgusted. "Sleep it off. And either be prepared to act as a team member, or go on home. I don't need you around if you can't be helpful."

"Helpful." Naomi got unsteadily to her feet. "That's right. We won't be kept on the staff if we aren't helpful. The queen has spoken. The goddamned queen has—"

Her voice thickened. She put one hand to her throat; her mouth opened and closed, working horribly. Her face contorted, her eyes bugged out. She fell back onto the couch, and then, as if in slow motion, onto the floor, striking the coffee table on her way down. Her body convulsed.

It seemed to last forever. I ran to crouch beside her. Her eyes rolled back, her mouth moved, but no sounds came out.

"Call an ambulance!"

Hannah, I saw, was petrified. Kim backed away, clutching the cloth she'd used to wipe up the spill. Her eyes were like saucers.

Naomi convulsed again. Froth appeared on her lips. I wanted to give her CPR, but she moved too much for me to get a grip on her. Her arms splayed wide, striking into the coffee table and the couch. I tried to hold her, to keep her from hitting her head or her body. Her convulsions were violent.

"Kim, call 911! Get help!"

"Right." She couldn't seem to look away.

"Now!"

She turned and fled. Naomi convulsed one final time, and was still.

I put a hand on her neck, then on her wrist. I felt no pulse.

Straightening, I looked at Hannah, who stood as if made from stone, her eyes wide and unblinking. Kim shouted into the phone in the foyer. Distracted, she hung it up. It began to ring.

"She's dead." I said it dully. Kim, sobbing, caught her breath. She clamped a hand to her mouth.

"No," Hannah said. "No. Not dead."

"I'm afraid so." I stared at Hannah. She was looking at Naomi, but she raised her head and caught my gaze.

"What?" She saw Kim watching her. "What are you looking at?"

"Nothing," Kim said, gulping.

"You think I killed her." Hannah turned to look at me. "You think so too. You both think I killed her, because she was writing a book."

"Not at all." I tried to sound soothing.

"How could I kill her? She must have had a heart attack." Hannah's voice rose. "It was a heart attack. You were standing right here. I couldn't have done anything."

"I'm going to be sick." Kim ran from the room, her shoulders heaving.

The phone rang on, unanswered. Hannah blinked and looked around the room, then swept her raincoat off the back of the couch where it had been draped. She clamped one hand around my wrist, reached into her handbag with her other hand, and pulled out a gun. It looked like a toy, but the metal on its sides gleamed dully, and somehow I knew it could do damage. "Come on," she said.

"What?" I wasn't functioning too well. I stared blankly from her to Naomi's body on the floor.

"Come on." Hannah pulled me impatiently into the kitchen. "Is this yours?" She pointed the gun at my knapsack, still keeping a tight grip on my hand. "Pick it up. You have a car, don't you?"

"Sort of." I took my knapsack off the table. "What are you doing? Why—"

"You ask too many questions." Hannah glanced through the kitchen door, into the beautiful drawing room, and drew a deep, shuddering breath. Everything in the room seemed to point at the still form beside the coffee table.

She swung the kitchen door shut and yanked me down the short hall that led to the freight elevator. "We'll go this way." She might have had twenty years on me, but she was taller, and very strong.

I could hear Kim upchucking in her bathroom as we rushed down the hall. Hannah pushed me out into the service hall and made sure the door was locked.

"Wait. This is a terrible idea. Why don't we stay and—"

"We're not staying." Hannah punched the button to summon the elevator and waited impatiently. I tried to tug my hand away, but she turned the gun on me.

"Don't give me any trouble. I could just shoot you and take your car."

"You don't even know what it looks like."

"I will soon." She waved me into the elevator when the doors opened. "I don't want to hurt you. But nothing gets in my way."

Under the circumstances, I didn't see what other choice I had but to go with her. Naomi was beyond help, and I didn't want to be shot and maybe killed. The gun looked very efficient, and given the perfect way she did everything else, I was sure Hannah was capable of killing me without further ado.

The freight elevator went all the way to the garage. It was cavernous and rattly, and the ride seemed to take forever. Hannah didn't speak. She watched me in an absent-minded kind of way, her thoughts elsewhere. I wondered if I could rush her when the elevator finally stopped, but her attention sharpened. She arranged her raincoat so it hid the gun, and gestured me out into the vast space of the garage. Her steely look was meant to remind me that she wasn't averse to shooting.

"Which is your car?"

I felt a bit of mean pleasure when I led her to the bus.

"This?" Her lip curled. "How the hell do you get into this thing?"

It flashed through my mind when I opened the passenger door for her that I could escape while she settled herself. But she gestured me to climb into the passenger seat ahead of her.

"Scoot on over." She followed right behind me, more agile than I expected—but then, she probably did weight training and yoga every day.

She kept the gun pointed at me while I scrambled into the driver's seat. "You are my escort, after all. So escort me out of here. Drive."

I drove.

9

THE parking attendant didn't seem to find anything unusual in me driving out such a short time after I had parked, accompanied by a woman whose face was familiar to the universe. I wanted to say something that would alert him to the fact that Hannah had her gun pointed at me, hidden from his view in a fold of her raincoat, but when I ventured a pleasantry she moved her hand closer to my side, and the look on her face made me quail. After all, she most probably had just killed her trusted, longtime associate. I assumed she would have no qualms about killing me.

The attendant waved me through in a bored way. I stopped at the exit onto California Street and looked at Hannah. "Now what?"

She hesitated, and at that moment we heard sirens approaching the hotel. "That way," she said, pointing away from the sound. "Move it."

I moved it. While I signaled, shifted, whipped the bus around turns, I pondered what to do. My mind was not working too well. I kept seeing Naomi crumple and fall to the floor. I could have sworn Hannah had looked as shocked in that moment as the rest of us.

We drove down California toward Chinatown. Ahead

the street narrowed and grew more congested. I had to stop for a moment behind a delivery truck parked in front of a small grocery store. The driver unloaded crates of glistening fish, their scaly bodies stacked like enormous sardines. Hannah moved impatiently as the driver engaged the grocer in an animated conversation.

I, however, welcomed every delay. At any moment, someone would recognize that the woman being driven past in the battered old VW bus was Hannah Couch. At least, that was my hope.

"So what are you trying to accomplish by this?" I took my attention from the traffic for a moment. "Flight is evidence of guilt, you know."

"I'm not fleeing." She stared straight ahead, but the gun was still pointed in my direction. "You're kidnapping me."

"No." I pulled across two lanes of traffic, while horns blared around me and angry drivers yelled from their cars, and turned onto Montgomery. "You aren't going to put this on me."

"Do what you're told or I'll shoot."

Ahead someone pulled out of a twenty-minute parking spot in front of a cappuccino place. I whipped into the spot, beating out a BMW, and killed the engine. "Go ahead. Shoot. I don't know how you'll blame me when I'm dead. And think, if it's possible. Kim is telling the police right now how you and Naomi fought all night. Don will substantiate it. My friend who's a police officer in Palo Alto will make it clear that I am not in the habit of kidnapping celebrities. You had better go back right now and face the music."

"Look." Hannah turned to face me. Her eyes were cold behind her spectacles, but somehow unfocused. I didn't think anything I said got through to her. "You are going to drive me around in this horrible car until I can think of a plan, a really good plan. I always come up with a good plan eventually. That's how I got where I am today. So drive, or I swear I'll jump out of this car, scream that you're kidnapping me, and have you thrown in the pokey so fast you won't be able to take a breath. I have powerful friends. Everyone in the world will believe me. Drive, or go to jail."

"I'm going to jail no matter what, because if I drive you, I'm an accessory in a homicide."

"No, you're not. There's no homicide." Hannah uttered this statement with supreme confidence. "Naomi killed herself, obviously. I'm just trying to get enough breathing space to figure out damage control."

I blinked. She was either self-delusional or she had multiple personality disorder. Either way, I didn't want to be at her mercy. "Hannah, every cop in the city will be looking for you."

As if to underscore my words, a ringing noise came from inside her handbag. She opened it, took out the cell phone, and turned it off. With a last beep, it was silent.

"The police won't expect to find me in this kind of vehicle."

"You'll be recognized no matter where you go." I was beginning to feel desperate.

She reached in her purse, took out a headscarf, and put it on. It transformed her from a fashionably dressed motherly person to a dowdy elderly woman. Nothing could disguise the designer clothes and shoes she wore, but with those hidden by her raincoat, she no longer looked like the famous Hannah Couch who had been on TV the night before.

"Satisfied?" She glanced at herself in the side-view mirror, craning her neck to get the big picture. "I don't always go out with an entourage. Naomi and I used to go to flea markets all the time, and no one ever recognized me."

There was silence while we both listened to Naomi's name reverberate through the car. Then Hannah flourished her gun again. "I'm putting this in my raincoat pocket, but it's trained on you. And let me just say that after my house was burglarized, I spent some time learning to shoot really well. At this distance, I can put a bullet through any part of you that I choose. Stomach wounds are supposed to be very painful to recover from." She pocketed the gun, and kept her hand in there with it. "So drive."

I drove. I pulled back onto Montgomery, crossed Market. Herded by the traffic, I found myself on Howard, veering into the left lane to avoid a lumbering truck, honked at by rushing Infinitis and Lexuses. I turned left onto Hawthorne; there was less traffic.

"I don't like this neighborhood." Hannah looked with disfavor on the grimy storefronts, the homeless winos rolled in their coats like bundles of dirty laundry, not yet awake to face the day. "Go that way." She pointed down Folsom. "Is that the bay?"

Would this turn into a kind of bizarre tour? "That's the bay." Turning left onto the Embarcadero, I headed northwest. The view out the big front windshield of the bus was a picture-postcard, even in midwinter. Morning fog was piled like whipped cream just beyond the Golden Gate; the early light showed the bridge against it in sharp relief. The water sparkled with whitecaps and the white sails of the occasional sailboat. Grape hyacinths bloomed beneath drifts of tulip trees growing out of large containers around Embarcadero Center. The stop and go traffic brought a welcome slowness to our progress. I hoped some alert policeman was even now phoning in a sighting of the missing Hannah Couch.

Although that wouldn't exactly benefit me. Hannah was right: if she claimed I kidnapped her, she'd be far more likely to be believed, especially given my past. No amount of clean living can wipe out an attempted-murder charge. I had finally gotten to a point in my life where I could forget about that part of my history, except when something raked it up again, something like being at risk for once more spending time in jail. I was not at all anxious for that.

I needed Hannah to turn me loose without involving me in whatever weird scenario had played itself out between her and Naomi. While we waited for the light at Battery, I tried chitchat.

"So why do you think Naomi killed herself? She doesn't—didn't seem like the type to me."

"Because no one else would have." Hannah still didn't look at me. From the corner of my eye I could see her staring straight ahead. She made no further comment on our route, even when I followed Embarcadero to its end in the heart of tourist territory, Fisherman's Wharf. Still no one seemed to recognize her; tourists were thin on the ground in January at seven-thirty in the morning. Shopkeepers hosed off their sidewalks, folded back their security gates, and got their stores ready for the day. None of them spared the bus a glance as we meandered past. "Naomi simply wasn't that important, no matter what she thought."

"I'm not sure I buy that." I swung up Taylor, turned

right on Beach. Souvenir shops lined the street on both sides. "You two went back a long way, didn't you?"

She was silent for a moment. Then, to my surprise, she answered.

"We were housemates at Smith." Her voice sounded younger, less assured. "I was on scholarship, and desperate for money. My family didn't want me to go to school; they thought I should have gotten a clerical job and brought home my paycheck like a good girl."

Again, she fell silent. We turned up Polk by Ghirardelli Square, along North Point, back down Van Ness. I drove as far as I could out the Municipal Pier. People were lined up for coffee at the kiosk near the bocce green. A mounted park ranger stared impassively over the heads of the crowd. The only way I could think to attract her attention was to ram her horse, and that seemed too drastic.

At the end of the pier I rolled down my window. The rush of cold, salty wind was like a slap in the face.

"What are we doing here? Keep driving." Hannah twisted in her seat, looking at the water on one side, the cliff of Fort Mason on the other side. Her hand moved nervously in her raincoat pocket.

"I wondered if we could hear the Wave Organ from here. It's around the point, but I think I can. Hear it?" Waves slapped the sides of the pier and crashed through the Wave Organ somewhere west of us, which emitted a hollow, groaning noise. I had always liked it, but now it seemed too macabre. "Never mind. I'll do you a big favor and show you one of my favorite spots in the whole world."

"This isn't a tour, you know." Hannah looked at me with disfavor when I turned the bus around and headed back up Van Ness to Bay. I swung into Fort Mason. "Where are you going? Is this some kind of police station?"

"Relax. It's part of the Park Service, not the army anymore, though they do have an officer's club over there somewhere." I drove down a little street, with old houses on it that dated back to the military's first presence in San Francisco in the late 1850s. Some of the houses were still occupied by army personnel; children scampered out a front door, intent on catching the school bus. "There's a youth hostel here. And something else very special." I parked the bus and opened my door. "Come on."

"I don't like this. What are you doing?"

"I'm showing you something." I turned and gestured. It made me very nervous, the way she fingered that gun, but I thought if I could loosen her up a little, get her to follow my lead, she'd eventually stop bossing me and come to her senses. "It's nothing to do with police or people in any way. Come *on*."

She climbed down from her side of the bus, managing to do so with her hand still in her pocket. "You are asking to be shot," she threatened, but she didn't do anything. At that moment, I felt my first tremor of doubt that she had killed Naomi. If she was ruthless enough to poison her longtime associate in front of witnesses, she was surely ruthless enough to shoot me and commandeer the bus.

Instead, she followed me along the path through the trees. I hadn't been to the spot in a long time, but it was still just as I remembered it—a small clearing in the thick vegetation, with a bench positioned to look out over the steep cliff that marked the end of Fort Mason. From the bench, a perfect vignette of the Golden Gate Bridge, the Marin headlands, and the distant buildings of Sausalito was framed by the surrounding greenery.

"Sit," I invited Hannah, doing so myself. "Take it in. It's very peaceful."

She sat, still pointing that stupid gun at me. The air was incredibly fresh, as if it had never been breathed before. It was impossible not to breathe deeply. I felt more relaxed almost instantaneously. I hoped its magic would work on Hannah too.

I could see her chest lifting. For a few minutes she didn't speak. I let the silence settle around us. If you were striving for clarity of thought, this was a good place to be.

Of course, it was also a good place to kill someone and leave the body.

I hoped that idea hadn't occurred to Hannah. I heard her breathing deepen and slow, and tried to project an aura of calm reflection.

How long we sat like that, I don't know, but after a while I heard a surprising sound—sniffles. Hannah was crying.

"Are you okay?" I groped in my pocket, but she was already patting her damp eyes with a hankie.

"I miss Naomi," she gulped. "She's been with me for nearly forty years. All that time, we had a common goal. I always thought it was the most important thing to her—really, to both of us. Why, she never even married, she was so intent on our work."

"How did you start out?"

At first I thought she wasn't going to answer my question. Then she put the hankie away and started talking.

"We were in Talbot at Smith. We ended up in the kitchen, cooking to earn our board." Hannah's lips thinned. "That's when I realized that most Americans don't have the foggiest idea of how to take good ingredients and make a meal, cookbook or not. I mean, even in the fifties, women were slavish devotees of Betty Crocker and mixes and instant foods. It was no wonder those girls liked my cooking; the previous cook had left a pantry lined with huge cans of soup and soggy vegetables and pie apples. They were so happy to get food that tasted real."

"Naomi worked in the kitchen too?"

"She also needed money. I had been on the verge of dropping out because even with a scholarship, I couldn't afford books or clothes, and she was in much the same straits." Her voice turned introspective. "My family wouldn't help me. In my father's opinion, college was a foolish dream. I could get a job in the local bakery, or for real class, an office job. I'd get married, and any education would be wasted once that happened. That's how it was done in his world. I was truly at the end of my rope, financially."

"So that was what led to the Roxy Ripper thing?"

She reared back, staring at me, outraged. Then, as quickly as it had come, her anger left; she sighed. "I only did it for a month. I was desperate, and so was Naomi. She didn't mention that in her nasty memoir. We both went down to try out when we heard they were hiring, but they weren't interested in her scrawny body." She stopped short and used the hankie again. "God, I hate sounding so awful. But she really made me mad, implying I did that for fun. Hell, I paid her board bill as well as my own before I quit."

"I thought you were in the dorm kitchen."

"After my brief and unlamented turn as a stripper, I got the cooking job." She was lost in her story, but not so lost that she forgot to point the gun at me. It seemed to me I was better off trying to talk her out of it than trying to take it from her. Something told me Hannah didn't like having things taken from her.

"And that was when you and Naomi started working together?"

"I needed a helper, so I offered the job to Naomi." Hannah shrugged. "We worked well together. She was smart enough to know when she didn't know something, and to follow instructions."

"Was your degree in domestic science?"

"No, accounting." She laughed. It was a rusty sound, as if not well used. "I was always good with numbers. But accounting was dull. My first job was in a stuffy firm in Boston. They didn't really approve of women working, and wouldn't have hired me if I'd been married." She snorted. "Girls today have no idea of what it was like to make your way back then. Kim thinks it's always easy to get a job that you enjoy doing. She hasn't got a clue."

"How long did you do accounting?" It occurred to me that if I got out of this alive, I would have the ingredients for a very special interview with the famous Hannah Couch, an interview that would sell for a very nice price to a prestigious magazine. Or, if Hannah ended up in jail, to a less-prestigious rag that would pay even better. I wished I had my notebook, or even the little tape recorder Drake had given me for interviews.

"Not long." She was relaxed, now. Still gripping the gun, but not as if it were surgically embedded in her hand. My mind raced in a different direction. Could I disarm her? If there was shooting at this range someone would get hurt, and it would most probably be me. I decided to wait to try anything drastic, unless things got much dicier.

"I got tired of crunching numbers for other people in

less than a year. And I had catered a couple of parties—one for Naomi's brother Tony's wedding, and one for someone in the office. I realized I had a gift for it. And it was far more rewarding. Naomi and I formed a catering company, and I resigned from the accounting firm. They were sorry—realized too late what they were losing." She laughed. I had been on the verge of liking her, but that unconscious arrogance nipped it in the bud. "They offered me a nice raise. But by then I knew what I wanted to do. And everything grew from that."

"So Naomi was your partner all along?"

"She never had much vision," Hannah said judiciously, "but she was great at executing. When I realized that ice sculptures would start a new craze, she was the person who found the one place left to get European-style ice sculptures. I'm going to miss her."

"So why did you cheat her over the crepe maker?"

She turned to me, her eyes wrathful. "Don't believe everything you hear. Naomi was getting greedy. She wanted to be a creative partner as well as a business one, even though mine has always been the guiding vision in our company. I commissioned that crepe maker with some other kitchen tools for a new line we're going to offer in our catalog."

"So she didn't invent it?"

Hannah took a few more deep breaths. "It's true that Naomi had one good idea about it. But she didn't design it alone. I did a lot of the work too. And she didn't build it—our contractor did. I gave her a very nice bonus for her contribution, but she wanted more." Hannah's jaw firmed. "If she hadn't killed herself, we'd have probably come to a parting of the ways. I was getting fed up with her need to be in the limelight."

Because that was your place, I thought, but had the brains not to say. Obviously Hannah would brook no competition at center stage.

Our solitude was disturbed by a man with a very large golden retriever, out for a morning stroll. The dog was interested in my pants legs, which probably smelled like Barker if your nose was very accurate. I scratched the dog's ears, earning a blissful look from the dog and a chatty "Good morning" from its owner.

Hannah stood up. "Let's go," she muttered, her hand once again in the raincoat pocket. I sighed and got to my feet. If our little interlude had been my opportunity to disarm my captor, I had blown it, so interested had I been in her recounting of tales from her past.

She marched me back to the bus, and once more had me climb into it from the passenger side, following me in quickly so I couldn't prepare any surprise for her. I drove back through Fort Mason while she fiddled with the radio, finally finding an all-news station. We listened in silence as a perky traffic reporter told us that traffic was sluggish on all approaches to the City. Several commercials followed. Then the news, full of depressing stories about blizzards, war, and Biblical-quality famine in various parts of the world.

"In local news," the radio chirped, "celebrity Hannah Couch is being sought for questioning in the suspicious death of her business partner, Naomi Matthews. The death occurred early this morning at the luxurious hotel where the two were staying while on a promotional tour for Ms. Couch's new cookbook."

"Cookbook!" Hannah was outraged. "*Hannah Hosts Brunch* is far more than a cookbook!"

"Shh." I turned up the radio. "Let's listen to this."

". . . believe she might have been abducted in connection with the death. Police are not saying if a ransom demand has been received, or if they have any leads on Ms. Couch's whereabouts. Her great visibility as a celebrity will no doubt help them find her.

"The threatened Muni strike—"

Hannah turned the radio off. "You see. They think I've been abducted."

"You didn't hear who they thought was kidnapped," I pointed out. "It might have been me."

Stopped at the Lombard Street light, we stared at each other for a minute. Ringing commenced again.

"I thought I turned that thing off." Hannah took out her phone. It was still off. The ringing continued. "Do you have a cell phone?"

The ringing was coming from my backpack. Hannah rummaged in it, found Judi Kershay's phone, and turned it off. The light changed.

"I need a better disguise," Hannah said worriedly. "Is there a BigMart around here?"

"The only one I know about is in Redwood City." I waited for it to occur to Hannah that the police would be looking for my bus. She didn't appear to realize that, and I wasn't going to enlighten her. Even if they thought I'd abducted her, it would get straightened out sooner or later once they'd stopped us and gotten the gun away from her.

"How far is Redwood City?"

"It's about thirty miles."

"We can't really stop at a phone booth to look in the phone book for a closer one," she fretted.

"Probably no phone book in most booths anyway."

"I guess we'd better go where you know to go," she decided. "Just get on the highway. Too many cops hanging around the city streets."

"If you say so." I headed straight down Van Ness, the lengthiest way to get on 101. "It'll take a while in all this traffic."

"Don't do anything stupid." She had her hand in her raincoat pocket again.

"I won't."

10

THE BigMart wasn't quite open when we got there. I parked as close to the front as I could on Hannah's instructions; on my own I like to park farther away, but I wasn't going to say anything. More people would see the bus up front, and maybe we'd be spotted. I had driven as slowly as I dared on the highway, hoping to be pulled over. When Hannah complained, I said that Babe wouldn't make it any faster. Since anything Babe does above fifty sounds like a lot of effort, with the rattling and the roar of the engine, she believed me.

No one had taken the least notice of the old VW bus with the two women in it. I began to think Hannah was right, and all middle-aged women looked alike to John Q. Public.

While we waited for the store to open, Hannah fidgeted nervously with the gun in her pocket. It gave me an uneasy feeling.

"What are you shopping for, anyway?"

She stopped fidgeting and looked at me. "You're coming too."

"I could just wait in the car."

She snorted. "Right. And leave me here. No, you're

coming in with me. And while I'm at it, give me the car keys."

I didn't want to. "You'll lose them, then we'll both be stranded."

"Maybe I'll just strand you." She thought about that for a minute. "You'd call the police, of course. They'd know what car to look for. I'd have to steal a different car, and I don't want to go to so much trouble. No, I'll just keep you here, driving for me." She looked around the bus with distaste. "No matter how old and nasty your car is."

"It's a classic," I said, defending Babe. "Over two hundred thousand miles, and still running fine."

"Fine?" Hannah's voice was heavy with disbelief. "Fine is how a Mercedes runs. Not this heap of yours." She held out her hand. "Pass over the keys."

I did so reluctantly. She put them in her other raincoat pocket, opposite the gun. I wondered if I could pick her pocket and get away without her knowing.

"The store is opening." I nodded at the big glass doors, which were being unlocked and pushed open. "What did you say we're shopping for?"

"Clothes. I'm going to change. And necessities. I might be on the road for a while."

"Look, Hannah, you can't just keep running. Sooner or later you have to face the police."

"No, I don't." She waited until I was on the ground before she climbed down. "At some point, they'll figure out that Naomi killed herself, and then I can go back."

She sounded supremely confident. It shook me. I was still positive that Naomi hadn't killed herself, because she had seemed, no matter how impaired by alcohol, to have a plan for revenge, and I didn't think the revenge was making it look as if Hannah had killed her. But if Naomi didn't kill herself, and Hannah didn't do it, who was left? Not Kim, surely. Naomi was her aunt, after all. Not Don, whose handling of any glass would have caused comment. It was impossible to know what had happened if Hannah had not been the cause of Naomi's death.

Hannah seemed to know what she was doing in the BigMart. I thought she must shop a lot cheaper than she needed to, before I saw the big display in the housewares section. "Let Hannah Couch Choose Your Dishes!" There was a cardboard cutout of the woman herself, wearing a homey apron and offering a pretty bowl of cookie dough. I had to admit, the dishes were nice, though nowhere near as cheap as Thrift Savers, the secondhand store in San Carlos where I get whatever kitchen tools and appliances I need. I don't need many, because I'm not a cook.

Of course, I immediately thought of the person who is a cook. Drake had been fixing me dinner most nights. He needed no additional gizmos of any kind. His kitchen was stuffed to the gills with gourmet accessories. It didn't get in the way of his cooking, though. Last night had been green curry chicken and vegetables with jasmine rice; he'd claimed it was simple, but it tasted wonderfully complex. I would have worried about becoming too dependent on his offerings if he hadn't made it clear he would cook dinner for me the rest of my life if I wanted. I hoped he didn't know that I was missing in action, perhaps even a suspect in a murder case. He hates that.

Hannah breezed past her cardboard twin without a glance. I took many glances, wondering if anyone would notice the striking similarities between the woman with the bowl and the woman in the headscarf and fancy rain-coat who pushed the hangers along the racks with single-minded intensity. Her choices, when she made them, were very sensible, just what I would have worn if I'd been fleeing a horde of police and fans: elastic-waist jeans, denim jacket, turtleneck, thick socks, and sneakers. She got a hairbrush and a toothbrush too.

"They have everything here, don't they?" My task was to push the shopping cart, while she followed behind me. "Maybe you could just get a new car while you're at it."

"It's a good value in here," she said rebukingly. "When they asked if I wanted to do a merchandising deal, I didn't hesitate. People need cheap things that are nice-looking. I use the line of serveware I developed for them myself. The dishes are pretty and durable, and if one breaks, it's easy to replace it."

I had been hoping that when we got to the checkout, she would pay with a credit card and the cashier would notice the name on the card. Of course, she was far more prepared than that. She had cash. According to Judi Ker-shay, celebrities usually didn't carry cash, but Hannah was not a typical celebrity.

"Shopping with your daughter? That's so nice." The checker was between my age and Hannah's. She folded the clothes and put them in a big bag.

"Yeah, this is Mom's first outing since the gallbladder surgery. Isn't it, Mom? You having fun?"

Hannah bared her teeth in a ferocious smile. "Yes, dear. So kind of you to bring me."

"You know, your mom looks just like Hannah Couch. Have you ever noticed that?" The checker peered in a friendly way at Hannah. "You could stand over there next to her picture and be her twin."

I opened my mouth to reply. Hannah beat me to it. "I hear that all the time," she said dismissively.

"Especially since you were ill," I added. "You used to be much better looking than her."

"Oh, I think she's a fine-looking woman." The clerk pushed the receipt into the bag and handed it to me, since my mom was too ill to carry things herself. "Probably has a lot of plastic surgery to stay that way, though."

"Bet she spends most of her time in bandages," I agreed.

"Thank you so much," Hannah said to the clerk. "Now, where are the bathrooms?"

"You don't want to wait too long in your condition." I was beginning to enjoy myself. "We'd better go now if we're going to get home okay."

The clerk pointed us to the bathrooms and turned to her next customer. I could hear her telling that woman what a close family we must be.

As soon as we were inside the rest room, Hannah locked the door and ordered me into a stall. "Lock it, and don't come out until I tell you to."

This was my chance. I listened to the rustling noises of her taking off her clothes, and figured I could rush her, get the gun and my car keys, and get away before she could get dressed enough to follow me.

I threw open the stall door and zoomed out. I had misjudged the time it would take her to change; Hannah was already dressed in the jeans and turtleneck. She was just putting the gun in the pocket of her new jacket.

"I didn't tell you it was time to go." She gestured with the gun. "But since you're here, you can put those things into the shopping bag. I won't be needing them."

She used the hairbrush and wiped off her makeup with

a paper towel while I crammed her clothes into the shopping bag and then, at her insistence, took them out and folded them neatly into the shopping bag. When she was done, she looked like any anonymous fifty-plus woman. Outside its usual bun, her hair straggled around her face, and without makeup, she looked more worn. She stuck her feet into the tennies and told me to tie them. I made the laces tight. I didn't want her to think I enjoyed my role as lady's maid.

The gun went into her jacket pocket. She slung her purse over her shoulder, gestured to me to pick up the shopping bag, and unlocked the restroom. I had thought someone might be waiting to demand an explanation for the locked door, but no one was there. We left the store, unremarked and unremarkable.

"Where to now?" I climbed into the bus and took the keys from Hannah. She settled herself on the passenger side.

"I need someplace to think, to just go to earth for a while." She frowned while I started the bus. "We could check into a motel, I guess."

"Not at ten A.M. They don't give rooms until the afternoon." I tried to sound knowledgeable, though I know nothing about motels myself. I always stay in the bus when I travel.

Hannah looked around with distaste. "I'd like a telephone. There isn't one here."

"You have one." I pointed to her purse, where her silenced phone reposed.

"I can't use that one." She sounded impatient. "You can easily trace the frequency and find out where the phone is being used. That wouldn't be smart, would it?"

"Who are you calling, anyway? The police?"

102

"My lawyer."

"There's a pay phone over there." I pointed to the corner of the parking lot, near the entrance onto El Camino.

"I won't be able to talk to him directly. I'll have to leave a message for him to call me back. Waiting at the pay phone wouldn't be smart either." She looked at me thoughtfully. "Don't you live somewhere around here?"

"I don't have a telephone."

She snorted with laughter. "You are a funny person, aren't you? I almost laughed out loud when you told that sales clerk I'd had gallbladder surgery." She nodded in decision. "We'll go to your house. Drive on."

"Hannah, this is a very bad idea of yours."

"Nonsense. I know just what I'm doing. It's the last place anyone will look for me." She gestured again with the gun. "Drive."

11

"**THIS** is your house?"

Hannah did not sound impressed. We had driven through the placid, tree-lined streets of Palo Alto, past the big old houses and the even bigger new houses, and she had gotten the idea that everyone who lived there was wealthy. Many folks have that idea. It's not altogether true.

"This is it." I pulled up the bus in front of the garage and put on the handbrake.

Hannah craned her neck to look back at Drake's house. A mow-and-blow crew came every week to keep his yard tidy, and the previous summer he'd had the house painted in yuppie colors of pale gray with peach trim, so it looked nice.

My house didn't look bad. I painted it myself, and touched it up when necessary; white paint with green trim, very traditional for a turn-of-the-century cottage. I had reshingled the roof, though I'd had to hire someone to come in and patch my patches. But I hadn't yet gotten the front porch fixed. In good weather my garden made up for any deficiencies, but everything was sleeping in January except for the calla lilies at the side of the house and the grape hyacinths and green shoots of daffodils along the walkway.

Drake's car wasn't in the gravel parking area between his house and mine. If he knew about the situation I'd gotten into, and police know most things, he didn't realize it had moved down to our place. I half hoped he'd never find out. I don't look for trouble at all. I only want a quiet life and time to garden and appreciative editors. I can't help it if other stuff happens. When it does, he tends to act as if I've brought it on myself some way. I'd like to know how I brought Hannah Couch on myself.

Hannah's sharp eyes noted every crack in the sidewalk, every loose board in the porch floor. I unlocked the front door, and Barker bounded out of the house to stand just in front of her, sniffing in that intensely personal way dogs do.

"Don't be rude," I said, not really meaning it.

"Too late," Hannah retorted. "Down, dog! Down."

"He's not up. Just tall." I snapped my fingers, and Barker backed off, regarding her with bright, interested eyes. He was still a puppy in many ways, though two years old. I wished that he was the kind of dog you could train to guard and attack. I fantasized about ordering him to hold Hannah, like a dog I had seen at a police demonstration one time, who had given the impression that if you moved any portion of your body, he would quickly bite it off. But Barker was a sociable fellow, ready to like everyone.

Hannah walked around my living room, her lips pursed. "Interesting," she said finally. "I see you have a Stickley chair."

"I do?" I followed her gaze to the shabby morris chair across from my equally shabby sofa. I usually sat in the other chair, an undistinguished overstuffed armchair with plenty of room for me, my feet, and my book.

"Yes, with the original finish, it looks like. You could get a nice little sum for that."

"What's 'a nice little sum'? Five hundred dollars?"

She looked at me with pity. "You should read more broadly, Liz. A signed Stickley"—she walked over and peered at the lower edge of the chair, then pointed out the signature to me—"goes for anywhere in the neighborhood of one thousand to five thousand dollars, depending on the finish. This one's in pretty good condition." She squeezed the top cushion experimentally. "And what feels like the original cushions and upholstery. Closer to the upper end, I'd say."

"Goodness." Right there in my house, I had the means to pay my property taxes. Of course, I'd have to find someone who agreed with Hannah about the value of my chair, and who would give me major bucks for it. That's always the sticking point with these collectible things. People will say how much they're worth, but no one steps up to hand over the money. "Do you want to buy it?"

"I'm not doing Arts and Crafts anymore," she said. "But I do know some dealers who might be interested."

I imagined her getting in touch with dealers from her prison cell, ordering them to check out my morris chair. It would never happen.

"Certainly you do a good evocation of shabby chic." Hannah looked at the couch, over which I'd thrown an old quilt to disguise upholstery flaws. I had inherited all the furniture when the two houses had come into my possession, and since it was all still usable, had seen no reason to spend my scanty resources on anything new. The friend who'd been the previous owner had taken good care of her things. Some of them, like the morris chair, must have come from her parents.

"I don't evoke shabby chic. I'm poor, and I have the furniture of a poor person. We do exist, you know."

She drew herself up. "Of course I know. I certainly wasn't born into a fortune. Everything I have, I've earned. That's why I'm not willing to let it all go up in smoke because Naomi"—she blinked and turned her head away—"because Naomi decided to take the coward's way." Her last words were muffled. She groped for her crumpled hankie, looked at it, and put it away.

I handed her my clean one. She snuffled into it, then looked at the monogram. "So what is your last name? This is an *M*."

"My last name is Sullivan. I get my hankies at the thrift store, with the rest of my linens." I grinned at her, trying to lighten the moment. "It's very exclusive."

She ignored the attempt at humor. "Can I have a glass of water?"

"Of course." I went into the kitchen and, for a special touch, put ice in a tall glass, which had also come from the thrift store. She followed me, sitting at the table. Her mental calculator was still running.

"This kind of table is collectible now," she said, examining the cherry-red top, the chrome legs. She pulled out one of the end leaves. "You've been using all this furniture? It's in such good shape."

"The woman who left it to me had only one child, no grandchildren." I spared a thought for Vivian, the sweet lady. Every day I blessed her. My cottage may not seem like much, but before it I was living in Babe, and indoor plumbing is the greatest advance civilization has made, in my opinion. I felt lucky to be under my own roof, most of the time. I did not feel lucky to have Hannah and her gun with me.

"That's a clever idea." Hannah nodded at my kitchen curtains. "Those old tablecloths are—"

"Collectible, I guess."

"Actually, they are, but you've cut them up, and the sun's probably faded them, so they're no longer desirable as tablecloths." Hannah drank some of her water. She didn't say anything about it being tap water, no lime, no fizz, but her face was expressive of her feelings. "They make nice curtains, though. Bright."

"I like them." I had a stack of Vivian's tablecloths, which I used on occasion for their rightful function, but their exuberant forties patterns of red apples, yellow bananas, and purple grapes seemed fitting for kitchen curtains at a time of low cash reserves. "You know, this collectible thing is like a made-up value. People see in your magazine and on your TV show that they've got something collectible, but nine times out of ten no one will give them anywhere near the money you're talking about. Don't you think that's a disservice?"

"Not at all." She sipped her water genteelly. Since it looked like she wasn't going to put a bullet through me anytime soon, I busied myself setting out food; I had gotten up very early that morning, and I was hungry. There wasn't much to eat, and I didn't feel like undergoing Hannah's scrutiny on anything I cooked. I'm not much of a cook, though I can get along okay. But anyone can make a peanut butter and jam sandwich, and when the jam comes from my friend Bridget's secret blackberry patch, it's fit for any number of media queens. As a sop to Her Highness, I trimmed the crusts off the bread and cut the sandwiches into fingers. Bridget actually did that to appease her horde of young children, but Hannah was pretty childish in some ways, so I figured it was worth a try.

She sniffed when I put the plate on the table, but I noticed she ate the fingers anyway. "I suppose that stove came with the house?" She pointed to my vintage Wedgewood, which I loved for its glistening white enamel finish and black accents, not to mention the chrome stovetop with built-in griddle.

"Actually, the stove came from the front house. The stove in this house had a bad gas leak, and my neighbor wanted to get one of those big fancy ranges, so he offered me this stove. It's been very nice. My neighbor," I added deliberately, "is a policeman. He'll be home for lunch, and when he sees my van, he'll be right over."

"Is he married?" Hannah appeared unconcerned. She helped herself to another finger sandwich.

"No."

She snorted. "You're just trying to frighten me, Liz. As if any single policeman would paint his house with peach trim." She glanced out the kitchen window, which showed the back of Drake's house. "Is he gay?"

I hoped she didn't notice my blushing. "No." During the past couple of months, I had had ample proof that Drake was vigorously heterosexual.

"You must think I'm an idiot."

I didn't answer that. I had warned her. If she chose to ignore my warning, it would be the worse for her. I just hoped no guns would come into play when Drake found us there.

Hannah used a paper napkin to clean off peanut butter crumbs. "Where did you say the phone was?"

"I said I didn't have one. I don't."

She looked incredulously at the kitchen walls and counters, as if a phone would materialize. "You really don't have a telephone? But—but how do you call people?"

"I use my policeman friend's phone. Or I go to a pay phone."

She considered. "I don't believe he's a policeman. I want to use his phone too."

I shrugged, took Drake's keys off the hook by the front door, and led the way down the walk and across the gravel parking area. The sun struggled feebly to break through the shrouding clouds. My roses looked menacing with their leaves stripped off, pruned into a two-foot-tall, thorn-studded hedge. I visualized shoving Hannah so she was impaled on them. She'd likely just get mad and shoot me, and it's not in my nature to cause anyone so much pain. Instead, I thought about spring arriving. Assuming I lived to see another spring.

Drake's kitchen was in good shape. He'd always kept it pretty clean, but the rest of the house had been a different story. Lately I'd been tidying the living room and bedroom, so all the mess had moved back into the spare bedroom. He didn't like for me to clean his house, but I couldn't help myself. Order is ingrained in me; it comes from living in confined spaces where if things aren't put away, there's no room to move.

The message light was blinking on his answering machine. I didn't bother to get the messages. One would be for me, from him, ordering me to stay put if I got there, and call him immediately. It was his response anytime trouble found me. I knew the drill. I just couldn't perform it.

Hannah nodded approval at the big commercial range,

the gleaming appliances, the cork flooring and copper utensils. "He likes to cook, obviously."

"He's a foodie." When we cooked together, I was in charge of vegetables. I was good with veggies. Drake handled the complicated main courses he loved to put together. "The phone's there."

Hannah dialed, and gestured to me to sit at the table a few feet away. Her hand was on the gun in her pocket again. I did as she asked, though I figured she would hardly shoot me when she was on the phone. I could dash out the front door and run to Bridget's house. Hannah was in good shape for a woman pushing sixty, but I doubted she could run faster than I could.

"David, this is Hannah. I am at—" She looked at the phone and then at me. I told her the number. The sooner David, whoever he was, called her back, the sooner I could put my plan into action. She gave David's voice mail the phone number, then hung up to wait.

"I want to hear the news," she announced. "Does your friend have CNN?"

"No idea. I don't watch much TV."

"What's the matter with you?" She seemed genuinely puzzled. "No phone, no TV. Are you a member of some kind of sect?"

"The Luddite sect? Not really. I just don't have time for it. I like to read."

She snorted. "Well, I bet your 'policeman' has a TV." She prowled into the living room and shot me a triumphant look when she sighted Drake's set. Although we watched movies on it in the evenings, I didn't know how to turn it on—he was in charge of complicated equipment. For all I knew he watched the news every

111

morning. Despite our close relationship, I didn't linger in the mornings. With Barker and my garden to tend, and, when I'm working at a temp job, my wardrobe to worry over, I had developed the habit of jumping up at daybreak to be on my way.

While Hannah searched for the remote control, I looked at the clock. It wasn't even eleven yet. So much had happened, it should have been midnight.

I took a deep breath and tried to concentrate on my dilemma. I had discarded the idea of trying to get the gun away from Hannah. Guns had a way of going off and causing damage.

Instead, I played through the idea of running away. It was the coward's way, but cowards are safe. I would run over to Bridget's, use her phone to call Drake, and tell him where to find Hannah. She would never be able to drive Babe in a million years, so she wouldn't be able to get far. Then it would all be over, and I could explain to Judi Kershay why everything had turned out so badly. I didn't relish that task, but I wasn't coward enough to duck it.

The TV squawked to life. Hannah punched buttons on the remote, looking for news. I inched toward the front door. It would be easier to get out the back door, but she might notice I was gone before I could get down the drive with its crunching gravel. The front door would give me a better start. I didn't think she would shoot me; that would cause a stir in the neighborhood.

". . . will bring pressure to bear through the International Monetary Fund for the present," the announcer boomed from the TV.

"Good. Here's the news." Hannah settled onto the couch. She pointed the remote at me, as if I too could be commanded by it. "You sit down. Stop hovering near the door. You make me nervous." She patted her pocket suggestively.

Obedient to the remote, I sank into a chair. At least it was close to the door. I went through it in my mind—the dash over there, the unlocking of Drake's two locks, getting down the steps and out to the sidewalk and far enough down the sidewalk to be out of her range of fire. The more I thought about it, the less I liked the odds.

"In other news, beloved lifestyle maven Hannah Couch has vanished after the suspicious death of her business partner, Naomi Matthews," the announcer intoned. A picture of Hannah posing with a bowl of cookie dough, looking much as she had in BigMart, filled the screen. Her motherly smile and apron made her seem like everyone's favorite grandmother. Looking at the picture, you might not realize what an out-and-out bitch she could be. "Police fear Ms. Couch was abducted by her driver, Elizabeth Sullivan." Another picture flashed on the screen. I blinked, hardly recognizing the mug shot taken of me nearly ten years previously. "Ms. Sullivan, who has a criminal record for attempted murder, was employed as a temporary driver during Ms. Couch's publicity tour, which was to continue today in California. Police are investigating both Ms. Matthews's death and the alleged abduction."

Hannah pointed with the remote control, and a deep silence filled the room. We looked at each other.

"Attempted murder?" Hannah's voice was casual, but I saw strain in her eyes. "Did you—are you the person who killed Naomi?"

"Don't be ridiculous." I jumped to my feet. "I barely knew the woman. I went to jail ten years ago for trying to kill my ex-husband before he killed me. That's why I don't like guns. I don't like people who take other people's lives. And you've really messed me up. I depend on temporary work, and who'll ever hire me now? You have a lot to answer for, Hannah Couch. How dare you ride roughshod over my life?"

She opened her mouth, but before she could speak, the phone rang. I made no move to answer it. After all, it wasn't my house. Hannah backed away from me, her hand in her pocket, and stood beside the answering machine until it clicked on. After a minute, I heard a man's impatient voice. "Hannah? Are you there? What's going on, anyway?"

Hannah snatched up the phone. "David. I—I just heard that I've been abducted."

"You mean you haven't?" Somehow she'd tripped the speaker phone button, and David's voiced invaded the room. "Woman, the police are looking everywhere for you. What on earth are you up to?"

"Well, I just had to—you know—get away." She sounded much less sure when speaking to her attorney. Perhaps he could influence her to stop this ridiculous scene we were involved in, before my last existing shreds of reputation were destroyed.

"Did that woman abduct you? Are you free? Because if you are, you must go immediately to the closest police station and tell them who you are."

"I wasn't abducted," Hannah admitted.

"Shoe's on the other foot," I yelled.

"Who's that? Is she there? Hannah, be careful."

"Ask her who's holding who," I shouted again. It was no time to worry about grammar.

114

"Be quiet." Hannah snapped at me, then spoke into the phone. "Look, David. I need you to get some kind of assurance for me, some kind of immunity."

"What are you telling me? That you killed Naomi?" David didn't sound too surprised. It must have occurred to him already.

"Not in the least," Hannah said, snapping at him now. "She must have killed herself. It's the only explanation. I want you to convince the police of that. Then I'll turn myself in."

"Where are you?" His voice was insistent.

"Why do you want to know?" Hannah's brows drew together. "Are you having this call traced? David, I trusted you. You're fired!" She slammed the phone down.

Again we regarded each other. "He's right. End this now. We'll go down to the police station. I'll ask Drake to take charge."

"No way." Hannah pulled the gun out of her pocket and looked at it. "So you've shot someone. Was it hard?"

"It was my life or his at the moment. And I didn't kill him. And it was awful. If you handed me that gun right now, I'd throw it in the creek or something." I didn't like the way her fingers tightened around the gun's butt. "Go ahead, shoot me. Then you'll be in real trouble, plus you'll have no transportation."

"You're right. If they were tracing that call, we've got to get out of here." She motioned me with the gun. "Let's go."

"Where? You're really jerking me around here. You've ruined my good name, and on national TV, no less. And now you're giving me orders. This really sucks, Hannah."

"Let's get out of here." She pushed me toward the back door. "We'll take your car."

115

"The keys are in my house."

She exhaled impatiently. "We'll get them. And any food you have. Let's go."

She stood at my kitchen door, directing me to bring the carrots, the cheese, the crackers. That was pretty much it in the food department. I wanted to rebel, but at this point, what good would it do me to get away? I'd just be arrested, and probably charged with Naomi's murder as well as abduction. It seemed to me my best course of action was to stay with Hannah until she ran herself into the ground, as would likely happen soon. Then maybe I'd be believed.

We got into the bus, and I started the engine. "Where to this time? The police station?"

She snorted. "Not likely. No, I know where I want to go. Your thrift shop."

"What?" I stared at her, amazed. "Did you say the Thrift Savers?"

"Why not? It's as good a place as any to hide out, and I collect antique linens."

Shrugging, I backed out, only to put on the brake as a car shrieked to a stop, blocking the end of the driveway. I hoped, prayed, that it would be Drake, and he would save me from the swampy morass in which I found myself.

It wasn't his car. It was Bridget Montrose's rusty old Suburban. Bridget hopped out, saw the bus, ran toward me. "Liz! Are you okay? What's happening?" She got to the driver's-side door, and looked across into the passenger seat. "It is Hannah Couch. My God! Did you really kidnap her?"

Hannah pulled the gun out of her pocket. "Not at all. I did the kidnapping. Now I'll have to take you along too.

We'll go in your car, in case they're looking for this one." She waved with the gun. "Get out, Liz. Your friend can drive. You sit in front beside her. I'll be in the back, with my gun."

12

I left the bus in the driveway instead of reparking in front of the garage. Hannah insisted that we get moving right away. The CNN report had freaked her out.

"I can't do this," Bridget said, while Hannah urged her toward her Suburban. "I have kids to pick up at preschool in a couple of hours."

"Let's go." Hannah showed the gun again. "I've just been asking your friend Liz here how it feels to shoot someone. Don't make me find out firsthand."

Bridget looked at me. I shrugged. Now that I'd been branded an abducting ex-con on national TV, I found myself less interested in attracting the attention of law-enforcement types. Drake would believe me, I knew, but any other cop who pulled us over would see me as the perpetrator because of my record, and that would be rather unpleasant until Bridget could verify my story. At this point, I would have been a total fatalist if it hadn't been for worrying about Bridget. If anything happened to her, I'd never forgive myself.

We climbed into the Suburban in the configuration Hannah dictated—Bridget and I in the wide front seat, Hannah in the middle seat. She had to push some toys out of the way and share the space with Moira's car seat.

Bridget turned to face Hannah. "You must see how ridiculous this is. I have children to tend. Liz needs her life back. We've done nothing to you. If you want to run away, why don't you do it on your own?"

"Drive," Hannah said. She sat, stony-faced, while Bridget started the car. It rumbled like an attack vehicle.

"When are you going to get a new car?" I listened to the various clanks and rattles, and wondered if we'd even make it to the Thrift Savers.

"I don't know. When Moira gets out of college, probably."

"But she's only two."

"Right." Bridget drove slowly up the street. "Do I have a destination, or am I just contributing to smog without any goal?"

"Hannah wants to go to the Thrift Savers and look for vintage linens."

Bridget looked at me in disbelief, then checked out Hannah in the rear-view mirror. "Is that right? You want to go to the secondhand store?"

"Of course it's true." Hannah put on her most haughty air. "As long as I'm forced into this distasteful role, I might as well see what I can find there. Perhaps it would make a good subject for our TV show."

"Delusional," I muttered. Hannah didn't hear me over the noisy engine, but Bridget did. "Humor her."

"I don't like this." Bridget's round face was pinched. Normally she is a sweet, sunny person who does whatever is put in her path and does it well.

"Nobody likes it. Certainly poor Naomi didn't."

Bridget was silent a moment, negotiating a turn onto El Camino. We went north, toward San Carlos.

"You think Hannah killed her?"

"I did at first." I glanced over my shoulder. Hannah was looking through the front windshield, her expression fixed. But I had no doubt that she could handle any rebellion we staged in an efficient and ruthless manner. "She rides roughshod over people, and murder is just an extension of that kind of personality. But now I'm not sure. She seems genuinely shaken and surprised, and it would have to be premeditated, unless Naomi just dropped dead of a heart attack or something."

"I hear what you're saying." Hannah's voice was curt. "You don't need to be talking."

"Well, if we can't talk together, why don't you tell Bridget about the book publicity trail? She's going to go on tour in a few weeks." If she didn't get killed by a homicidal homemaker, anyway.

"Really? What did you say your name was?"

"Bridget Montrose. My book just came out a few weeks ago."

"Oh, yes. I remember reading something about it. You popped onto the bestseller list after a very good review in the *Times*." Hannah looked at Bridget with more interest. "I have bought your book, of course. I hope to read it sometime. So you're going on a book tour."

"Yes. My publisher has arranged it. They wanted me to go for two or three weeks, but I explained I have small children and they crammed all this stuff into ten days. There won't be time for laundry, and I don't have that many clothes anyway."

"Perhaps we should be shopping for Bridget's travel wardrobe." I said that as a joke, but Hannah picked up on it in all seriousness.

"You can get a personal shopper at Nordstrom to help you with that."

"Can I get a personal checking account from them too, to pay for it?" Bridget gestured around the inside of the car. "We are going to remodel our house as soon as we get permits, and there's nothing extra in the budget for a Nordstrom wardrobe. Thank goodness the publisher's paying for the book tour. If it was a choice between that and new cabinets, I would definitely go for the cabinets."

Hannah waved these petty annoyances away. "Get a nice, basic skirt and pants, a couple of jackets, and comfortable shoes. Two or three shells or blouses. Make sure the fabric travels well—microfiber is good to resist wrinkles. Hotels will clean your clothes at night. Scarves and other accessories freshen the look. It's all in last July's issue of my magazine, when we talked of travel. Take along exercise clothing. You do exercise, don't you?" She leaned over the seat back to eye Bridget's rather ample figure.

"I exercise when I have time."

"You'll have to make some time in the mornings, because it really helps you cope with the stress of being on tour. Eat lots of salads, dressing on the side. Drink lots of water. Your driver can buy it for you."

"Treat your driver well," I said, glaring at Hannah. "Don't abduct her and her friends."

"I'll definitely remember that one."

"Look," Hannah said, with what passed for patience. "I don't want to be the bad guy. I don't want to frighten people. But you don't understand. I can't be arrested and questioned, and have suspicion thrown on me. It would ruin everything I've worked for." She sounded defensive. "I did the best thing under the circumstances. They're sure to figure out how Naomi really died, and then it will all blow over. If I'd been there, it would have turned into some kind of media circus."

"And it's not now?" Bridget raised her eyebrows. "It's all over the TV. Plus, you've ruined Liz's reputation. All that old stuff will be dragged out, all those other murders—"

"Other murders?" Hannah turned to me. "You said you didn't kill your ex-husband."

"He wasn't my ex at the time."

"I'm sure he's glad to be now."

"He's dead." I didn't want to have to go into all this. "Look, I didn't kill him. He was a scumbag, and someone else killed him later. I didn't kill any of them."

"Any of whom?" Bewildered, Hannah looked from me to Bridget. "You're a mass murderer?"

"Not at all." Bridget spoke up stoutly. "Liz has actually figured out some murders."

"And not figured out others—not nearly soon enough." I didn't like the direction the conversation was taking. "Look. There's the Thrift Savers."

"Why don't you figure out this one, then? Save us all a lot of trouble." Hannah ignored the big building with shelves of glassware sparkling in the windows. She was intent on me now.

"I thought you said Naomi killed herself. Now you're saying she was murdered. Which is it?"

"I thought she did kill herself. She was miserable, and it would have been like her to think she would succeed in mixing me up in scandal by making it look as though I did it. But maybe it was someone else. Someone who wanted her out of the way badly enough to kill her." Hannah shivered, losing some of her iron control.

"You know what that means," I said, while Bridget

parked in the lot behind the Thrift Savers. "Someone in your entourage."

"I know." Hannah fell silent.

"Well, here we are." Bridget spoke brightly, but her eyes were worried. "Are we getting out?"

"Of course. I never miss an opportunity to comb through the secondhand stores." Hannah gestured with the gun. "I'm keeping this in my pocket, so don't think you can get away with anything. The two of you stay just ahead of me. I don't want to hurt anyone. But I always do what has to be done, and I am a crack shot."

Inside the Thrift Savers it smelled of old upholstery and dust. Usually when I'm there I check the towels and washcloths; I've found things that have hardly been used. I look at the plates and glassware too. I like interesting plates, so long as they don't cost more than a dollar, and have amassed a collection of the kind with a landscape picture on them. If a glass or plate breaks, it doesn't matter, because there are more at the Thrift Savers.

Bridget and I became Hannah's linen slaves, searching through the stacks of tablecloths and place mats and napkins for those distinguished enough to belong in her collection. I found a hankie embroidered with a little cowboy boot and cactus and wouldn't let Hannah have it. "No, I found it," I insisted. "It's mine."

Hannah pouted. "You can come here anytime. I'm only here this once."

"And so is this hankie. It's mine." I clutched the treasure to my chest and glared at her.

She shrugged. "Be that way."

"Children, don't quarrel." Bridget spoke absently. She had strayed over to the nearby bookshelves instead of cruising the linens. "Here's something really interesting.

A first edition of Sue Grafton's *A Is for Alibi*. I thought everyone knew how valuable this is."

"It's valuable?" Hannah eyed the book. It was worn and missing its dust cover, but unmistakably Sue Grafton's first Kinsey Millhone.

"Not as valuable as if it was in fine shape. But it'll fetch a few hundred, probably." Bridget tucked it under her arm. "This one's mine. Travel wardrobe, here I come."

"Didn't you get a good advance for your book?" Hannah stopped shopping long enough to quiz Bridget. "And of course the bestseller list means royalites."

"Months from now." Bridget looked gloomy. "Everyone thinks you make a lot of money writing, and maybe *you* do," she told Hannah. "I was happy with my advance—some of my friends who write novels get only half as much. But if you look at it as a year's salary, it sucks. And it still wasn't enough to remodel the kitchen, especially after the agent's fee and the estimated taxes came off the top. They're offering me a lot more for my next book, but I won't sign anything until I know there'll be a next book." She closed her lips tightly; I guessed that she hadn't meant to say so much. Only to a couple of her writer friends had Bridget confided that she was not getting anywhere with her attempts to write another novel. She had thrown away several promising beginnings because they didn't move forward. We didn't mention the dreaded *b* word (block), but she spent more time with contractors and the city planning department now than she did at her keyboard.

"Well, maybe you should write a mystery." Hannah nodded at the book tucked under Bridget's arm. "Then yours would be worth hundreds someday."

"They're too hard to write."

"You're better at solving mysteries than I am." I had to put in my two cents' worth.

Hannah planted her hands on her hips. "Do you all do nothing but deal with murdered people? That does it. You're going to solve this one so I can get back to work."

She marched us up to the cash register to buy the hem-stitched damask tablecloth she'd found. Bridget and I paid for our items. Bridget earnestly told the cashier that next time, they should keep back the books that were worth a lot and sell them themselves, but the cashier just looked at her blankly.

"Now," Hannah announced when we were back in Bridget's car, "we're going to sit here until you solve this crime. If you're both so used to doing it, that shouldn't pose any problem."

Bridget and I looked at each other. If we stayed in the parking lot long enough, either the San Carlos police would come to give us a parking ticket or the tow truck would come to take us away. Either way, we'd be out of Hannah's frying pan and into the uncertain fire of police custody.

"Okay," said Bridget. She folded her arms across her chest. "Start by telling me the whole story."

"Wait a minute." Hannah looked around. "Someone may notice us parked here."

"You think?" Bridget shrugged. "Probably not."

Hannah narrowed her eyes. "We'll go to your house," she said finally, waving the gun in Bridget's direction. "They might be looking at Liz's house."

Bridget started to say something, but I poked her. If Hannah knew that her house was only a couple of blocks from mine, and that people were constantly coming and going, she might decide to really go to earth.

Beneath the rumble of the Suburban's engine, Bridget said to me, "I don't like this one bit. I don't want her waving that gun around at my house."

"The kids aren't there, right? Someone will see her or come in and recognize her, and call the cops. Better than having her decide to rent a motel room for the duration."

"I guess." Bridget drove down El Camino, her brow creased. "So if the fastest way to get rid of her is to solve the crime, why don't you fill me in on what happened?"

So that's what I did on the drive back to Palo Alto.

13

BRIDGET'S house was one of the Victorian bungalows that used to be far more prevalent in Palo Alto before people decided to tear them down in favor of monstrous lot-hogging fortresses. She and her husband, Emery, were committed to fixing their old house, but everything cost more in a rehab, so progress had been slow. They had gotten so far as to paint the outside and reshingle the roof. It looked very nice from the street.

Bridget pulled the Suburban into the drive and turned around to face Hannah. "I have a no-gun policy in my house," she announced. "Even toy guns are frowned on. Yours is not a toy."

Hannah appeared to find this amusing. "Didn't you say you have sons? I can't imagine little boys playing without guns."

"Well, your imagination needs work." Bridget crossed her arms. She and I both knew that her boys made weapons out of everything that crossed their paths. But Bridget still held fast to her rules. No toy guns in the house, and any visiting guns were put away until it was time for their owners to go.

"Well, I won't give up my gun." Hannah scowled. "I need it to keep you from interfering with my plan."

"You don't have a plan," I said brutally.

"And you don't need the gun," Bridget added. "Liz has told me the story. I'm not sure how much help we can be to you, but I'm willing to take a stab at it. Though I think the police would do a much better job of figuring the whole thing out. They probably already know the cause of death, which we don't."

"Yeah," I chimed in. "Maybe it was natural, and this whole thing is for nothing."

Hannah didn't like my comment. "Naomi was healthy as a horse. We just had our yearly checkups. She did the office workout every morning, like the rest of my staff. Believe me, that was not a natural death."

"Okay, I believe you." Bridget made her voice soothing. "But you still don't need the gun. If you'll take responsibility when the police find out and want to charge us as accessories or something—"

"And they will want to do that," I muttered.

"I will gladly clear my schedule for the next few hours and sit down to go over everything."

Hannah thought for a minute. "I'll put the gun in my purse, which is where I always carry it. If we'd met under other circumstances and you'd invited me into your home, you would never have known about it."

Bridget appeared to accept this tortuous logic. We went inside.

The inside of Bridget's house didn't measure up to the outside. The floors were scuffed, with finish worn off in spots. The kitchen was still as it had been forty years ago, with the exception of the microwave oven perched on one counter. Nevertheless, the whole house exuded a welcoming warmth that no amount of paint and polish could create.

Bridget went straight to the telephone. "I have to arrange child care," she told Hannah, who'd made an alarmed grab for her handbag. "I'm not going to fink on you, no matter how much I think you should just go to the police."

Hannah stood over her while Bridget dialed. "Melanie," Bridget said into the receiver, "could you pick up Mick and Moira and keep them this afternoon? I'll be glad to reciprocate next week."

I could hear Melanie Dixon's high, carrying voice from where I stood in the kitchen doorway. She would be consulting her enormous book of appointments and finally, after impressing Bridget with how busy and important she was, she would confirm that the Salvadoran woman who looked after her own two girls would be equal to the task of looking after Mick and Moira also.

Moira loved to play with the Dixon girls. I'd picked her up there once after a play date, and she'd been very reluctant to relinquish a pink, frilly ballerina doll. At home, the taste in dolls ran heavily to cartoon action figures, which Moira appeared to enjoy engaging in violent pretend games as much as her brothers did. But when there was pink around, she wanted it.

"Thanks, Melanie. What? Oh, something's come up. I'll tell you about it later."

She dialed again, this time a mom in her older son Corky's class, and arranged for Corky and Sam to play after school.

Hannah was taken with the dial phone. "This is marvelous. Where did you find it?"

Bridget raised an eyebrow. "We had it put in when we moved here some twenty years ago. It wasn't particularly cutting edge then, and Emery wants to replace it."

"Oh, no." Hannah wiped a smudge off the red plastic casing of the wall phone. "You mustn't do that. This is—"

"Let me guess. Collectible." I looked at Bridget. "Like everything in my house, evidently."

"Well, you do live in a time warp," Bridget pointed out. "No phone, no TV, no e-mail, no Jacuzzi—"

"You don't have a Jacuzzi either, or a dishwasher, or a garbage disposal."

"Yes, but I want them," Bridget admitted. "You don't."

Hannah marched over and sat at the kitchen table, clutching her purse to her midsection. "This is fascinating," she said in the polite voice that contradicts its words, "but it doesn't have anything to do with our problem."

"Your problem." Bridget put the kettle on.

I got out the teapot and chose a calming green tea blend, while Bridget rummaged in the pantry and came out with a plate of cookies. "I hesitate to serve Hannah Couch anything," she said, putting the plate on the table. "No doily, and they aren't fresh baked. I made them yesterday."

"I'm surprised there are any left." I took one eagerly. Bridget's oatmeal raisin chocolate chip cookies were always acceptable in my book.

Hannah took one, turning it over analytically before she bit in. "Interesting combination," she said. Then she stopped analyzing and ate the cookie. I had another, and so did she.

Bridget plunked the filled teapot and some cups onto the table, and fetched a pad of paper and some pens. "I think better when things are written down," she said, uncapping her pen. "Now, we are supposing that Naomi's death was murder."

"Right." Hannah watched Bridget writing. She reached into her handbag, and Bridget and I froze for a moment, before she pulled out a thick leather-bound agenda, the kind that says serious scheduling goes on. She opened it and took out a Cross pen and prepared for jotting down her own inspirations. I felt left out, but my notebook was in my knapsack near the door, and I didn't want to wander away in case I needed to protect Bridget from any sudden moves Hannah might make.

"So if you didn't kill her, and Liz didn't kill her, that leaves who?"

Hannah stirred uneasily. "That's just the problem. It couldn't have been Kim, because Naomi was her aunt."

"But didn't you accuse Naomi of causing her brother's death? Seemed to me Kim was very close to her uncle."

Hannah tapped the pen against her closed lips. "I did say that," she admitted, then scowled at me. "You must have been eavesdropping."

"So you said it, but you didn't mean it."

Hannah's gaze slid away. "Look, Naomi said things she didn't mean too."

"She said you fed your husband poison mushrooms."

Bridget scribbled busily.

"Don't write that claptrap down," Hannah commanded. "We were arguing. Words were spoken in the heat of anger."

"I'm writing everything down," Bridget added. "Sometimes it's the smallest things that lead you to the solution." I caught her eye and she glanced away. "At least, that's what Inspector Gadget says."

"Who?" Hannah looked confused. "I told you, no police. We'll get to the bottom of this without them."

"Right." I thought this was futile. We didn't have the resources to figure it out. But I would play the game. "So Kim might have thought Naomi poisoned her favorite uncle. You thought she was writing a tell-all book about you—"

"I know she was." Hannah's lips tightened. "She sent me pages out of it, where she talked about the past in a very unflattering way."

"The part about Roxy—"

"Don't go there."

Bridget was curious. "Roxy who? What?"

"It's nothing important."

"It's not important now," I pointed out. "Now that Naomi is dead and you can keep anyone from finding out. Unless she had her manuscript with her, in which case the police have already found it and figured that into your motive."

"I don't have a motive!" Hannah threw her hands into the air. "I keep telling you. None of this mattered. I could always squash anything Naomi tried to do, and she knew it. Besides . . ." She stopped talking, looking from one to the other of us.

I felt as if Bridget and I were the jury, sitting in judgment of Hannah while she had to drag all the tawdry bits of her life out and justify them for us. There is a certain amount of power attached to feeling like that, but I didn't care for it. The whole thing was starting to make me want a shower.

"Besides what?" Bridget was made of sterner stuff. She meant to get to the bottom of this and reclaim her life.

"I found her manuscript. Last night, when she was

dead drunk." Hannah spoke in a rush, the words tumbling out as if it was a relief to her to let them go. "She had it in her suitcase, and I found it and sent it down the hotel's incinerator chute."

Bridget and I looked at each other. "Was it computer generated?"

"What?"

"Had she written it on a computer? If so, it's still on her hard drive, and maybe copied on a disk." Bridget spoke patiently, as befits a Silicon Valley resident to a member of the technically challenged class.

Hannah brushed these objections away. "It was typed, but the only computer Naomi has is in her office at Couch Productions. I can secure that with one phone call." She started to reach into her handbag, then remembered that her cell phone was turned off for the duration. "Damn."

"You can't call from here, either," Bridget said. "Unless you want them to know where you are. The police have probably got every phone you might call under surveillance."

I had a moment's chill. Would they have done that to her lawyer's phone? Did they know that Hannah had called him from Drake's line? That might be very bad for Drake. I would hate it if he got into trouble because Hannah made me let her use his phone.

"Well, no one will think to go into her computer." Hannah seemed uneasy, though.

"And probably the police have already commandeered it. Probably they're the only ones going through it."

Hannah thought about that. Her mouth folded down.

"My advice, for what it's worth," I said, "is to write your own memoir, and just say very frankly that you were driven to exotic dancing for a brief period before you realized you could make your way through college by cooking."

Bridget's eyes grew round. "You were an exotic dancer?" She looked Hannah up and down. "That's a compliment, in a way. You're very attractive now, so you must have been a knockout when you were younger."

Hannah was still glaring at me for letting the cat out of the bag. She brushed Bridget's comment away. "It's not the kind of thing I want to be questioned about in an interview, and believe me, everyone wants to dig up your dirt in an interview."

"At any rate, no one would kill to keep that quiet. It's no big deal in today's world." Bridget spoke briskly. "I'd be more worried about her saying that you killed your husband with poison mushrooms."

"I did not." Hannah clutched her handbag closer. "I loved Morton. He was a good man. He really helped me get my career off the ground. He never held it against me that I couldn't have children. We were happy."

Bridget raised her eyebrows at me. "If you say so. How did he die, then?"

"It was something he ate," Hannah admitted. "He had been on a business trip, and he would eat in the little dives, no matter what I told him. He was sick when he got home, and nothing I could do helped. I insisted he go to the hospital, and finally he went, but it was too late— he had a heart attack brought on by his extreme dehydration." Tears glistened in her eyes. "He was my best friend, more than Naomi. My only friend, really. Now they're both gone."

She put her handbag on the table and scrabbled inside it for a hankie. Bridget patted her shoulder sympathetically. "That's hard on you. Let's get this finished so you can get your life together again."

"I would never have killed either of them." Hannah dabbed her eyes with the handkerchief. "I don't have many friends. None, actually. I've been too busy to worry about friends, and frankly, it's easier to be the boss if you don't cozy up to the underlings." She sniffed.

The front door opened and a voice called, "Bridget? Yoo-hoo."

Hannah sprang up. "Who's that?"

"It's Claudia," Bridget said, glancing at me.

Claudia was already talking. "I'm worried about Liz," she said, just before she appeared at the kitchen door.

Claudia Kaplan, one of Bridget's friends, had helped me out a few years earlier, at a very tense time in my life. One of a circle of writers Bridget and I knew, she had published some well-received and popular biographies of notable women. She looked queenly as usual, her graying hair pinned up with a variety of combs, her tall frame swathed in woolly layers surmounted by a huge turquoise and red shawl.

"I'm okay, Claudia."

She stopped, looking from me to Bridget, to the interloping Hannah Couch, who stood against the wall, pointing a gun at her.

"What's this mean? I thought the news must have had it totally wrong when they said you kidnapped Hannah Couch." Claudia finished unwrapping her shawl, her composure not the least ruffled by being held at gunpoint.

"It was wrong. Backward, you might say. Hannah abducted me, then Bridget."

Bridget looked sternly at Hannah. "We had an agreement. Put the gun away, or you can't stay here."

Hannah was confused. She waved the gun. "All of you, sit down."

Claudia gave me a meaningful look; I got her message. We closed in on Hannah, one on either side. Her gun waved wildly between us. "Sit down, I say. I will shoot."

"Why will you shoot? We're helping you, aren't we?" Bridget spoke in her reasonable, child-managing voice. "Just put the gun away and let's get on with it."

Hannah decided to train the gun on Bridget. "Both of you go sit down, or I'll shoot your friend."

This made me very angry. Bridget didn't deserve to be threatened. She was trying, in her usual generous way, to help.

Claudia and I exchanged looks again. "Hannah!" Claudia's bellow was loud and imperative. Hannah swung toward it instinctively, and I leaped at her arm and yanked it to the ground. The gun went off.

"Damn it." Bridget was on her feet. "I told you all, no gunplay. This has gone far enough."

"Yes, it has." My ears rang. Using Claudia's shawl, I picked up the gun. It had hit the floor half a second after the shot.

Hannah stood there, stunned, her arm hanging limply, fingers relaxed. Claudia appeared intact, as well. The room was full of a sharp, smoky smell. A neat, round bullet hole had appeared in the floor.

"So how does it feel to shoot at a room full of people?" Claudia put her hands on her ample hips and glared at Hannah. "You could have killed someone."

"You should have sat down," Hannah whispered. She examined her empty hand, then put her fingers to her lips. "You should all have sat down when I told you."

"We should have," I agreed. It gave me a terrible feeling to think that Bridget or Claudia could have been hurt. "Let's do it now. Bridget, do you have a plastic bag or something?"

Bridget found me a plastic bag and put the kettle on again. Claudia led Hannah to the table and pushed her into a chair. "Sit. Don't make more trouble." She looked at Bridget, at me. "What in the name of all the muses together has been going on here?"

I tucked the gun into a plastic bag and took it to the only place in Bridget's house that locked—the filing cabinet in her office. After a moment's thought, I put the filing cabinet key on top of the tallest bookcase in the room, which required me climbing on a chair to reach it. Then I did something I knew would make Claudia and Hannah hate me. I used the phone on Bridget's desk and punched in the number for Drake's private work line.

Of course I got his voice mail. I whispered, "Drake. I'm okay. Hannah made me go with her, and we've ended up at Bridget's. Hannah's been disarmed and we're all safe. The others don't want me to call you until we've figured out what's going on, but I wanted to let you know I'm all right."

I hung up the phone gently, hoping that some good would come of my call. I didn't know how often Drake was picking up his voice mail, but I was willing to bet, with me in trouble again, pretty often.

When I got back to the kitchen, Bridget had filled Claudia in on the morning's events; she had also filled the teapot and cookie plate.

Claudia ate her way through a cookie while she looked at Bridget's page of notes. Hannah seemed shrunken sitting there. I poured her a cup of tea, and she seized the warm cup gratefully in trembling fingers.

"Excellent," Claudia said, slapping the notepad back onto the table. "Okay, let's get back to it. I'll help."

Hannah roused herself. "Aren't you going to call the police now?"

"We should." I wanted the legitimacy of telling them I'd already done so, but I couldn't bear to hear the resultant outburst from Claudia and Hannah, both with powerful lungs, both unafraid to use invective.

"Not yet," Claudia protested. "I haven't gotten to play Nancy Drew yet. Let's figure it out, then we can just hand it to the police, a fait accompli."

Bridget pursed her lips. "I did get rid of the children for the afternoon, so we have until four or four-thirty."

"Shouldn't take that long." Claudia hitched her chair closer to the table. "So where did you leave off?"

Hannah glanced around the table. "You're not turning me in," she said slowly. "After I forced you to go with me, and even shot at you, you're going to help me?"

"Just call us stupid," I said with a little bitterness.

"No. I can think of a lot of names for you all, but stupid isn't one of them." The first genuine smile I'd seen from her blossomed on Hannah's face. "Thank you. Thank you very much."

"Don't thank us yet," Claudia said. "Wait till we actually figure it all out. Here. Have a cookie."

138

14

"I like Kim for it," Claudia said, chewing on the end of the pen. "She heard you say that Naomi had killed her uncle, and she wanted revenge."

"But that runs into the same problem. How did Kim kill her, and why was she carrying some kind of poison around?"

Hannah listened to us as she had for the last half hour, like a spectator at a three-way tennis match. Claudia was a vigorous player, lobbing many wild hits; Bridget knocked them all down with forceful sweeps of logic.

Undeterred by all the talk of poison, Bridget put down a plate with the cheese I'd brought from my house, some crackers, and a bowl of apples.

Hannah looked at the arrangement critically. "You can get beautiful paper cheese leaves through my catalog, dear. They are especially nice when you're serving a soft goat cheese or a Brie like this."

"It's not Brie." Bridget stuck a little spreader in the top of the cheese she'd added to my more pedestrian cheddar. "It's *fromage d'Affinois.*"

"Hmm." Hannah tried some on a melba toast. "It's very nice." She used my pen to write the name on a piece of paper from my notebook, which she tucked into her handbag. "You're not getting anywhere, are you, dear?" Her voice when she spoke to me carried the same hint of criticism. "Lovely doodles."

I was doodling, and trying to summon Drake with mental telepathy. It was taking him a lot longer to respond to my message than I'd thought. I wondered if he was just washing his hands of me and turning it all over to the San Francisco police, who'd have to drive down in heavy traffic to secure our band of intrepid amateur detectives.

In fact, none of us were getting anywhere. I munched on a cracker spread with the *fromage*, which was so creamy it seemed as if the cow could have produced it without human assistance. Bridget refilled the cookie plate. It was getting late.

"If it comes to that," I said, "why would anyone carry poison around?"

Hannah looked up from the apple she was peeling. "Naomi might have brought poison, if she meant to kill me."

We were all silent for a moment. "Did she?" I ceased doodling to write down Naomi's name, with three significant underscores.

"I thought she might." Hannah shivered. "I thought, if she'd killed Tony, nothing would stop her from killing me."

"What made you think she'd killed—Tony?" Claudia consulted her notes. "Her brother?"

Hannah nodded. "He was actually very good at running our gourmet take-out operation. Better than either of us would have been on a day-to-day basis. He trained his staff well too. I used him to cater a number of events, and he always did a fine job."

"So she killed him because he was good at what he

did?" Claudia shook her head. "That doesn't sound plausible."

"He wanted to buy it, and Naomi was really digging in her heels."

"He'd be more likely to kill her, in that case." Claudia made a note.

"They were having screaming matches over it." Hannah shivered. "Naomi just wouldn't hear of him buying it. She liked to lord it over him because she was successful, and he was just riding her coattails. He called her some terrible names too. One day they had a really bad fight, and the next day, he dropped down dead. Everyone said it was his heart, that he'd had heart trouble before. But Naomi was so . . . triumphant. That's when I thought she probably killed him."

"She made him have a heart attack?"

"It's possible." Hannah sounded defensive. "She majored in chemistry. She's always been interested in chemical reactions. When we first started out as caterers, she was the baker."

We were all silent for a minute. I doodled some more, and realized I was writing Kim's name.

"I can't believe that Kim had anything to do with it," I said, staring at my page. "She's just not the type of person to murder someone."

"All types commit murder," Claudia said with authority. She fancied herself a criminologist, and kept a certain rivalry going with Drake in that respect. It was true that she had a first-class brain, but she didn't always know as much as she thought she did.

"But not Kim," I argued. "She's not even twenty, for crying out loud. She's . . . obedient, for lack of a better word. She takes orders. I don't think it would even occur

141

to her to kill someone. And she was looking forward to the tour. This pretty much ends the tour."

Hannah rooted in her handbag and brought a hankie to her eyes. Counting the one I'd given her, she'd gone through three hankies. "I guess it does," she said, her voice muffled. "I thought I could just go on. I thought we would have to pick up our schedule. But I can't go on without Naomi. I know we fought, but she meant so much to me."

I had decided that Hannah was innocent of Naomi's death, but this speech made me reconsider. I looked at her with narrowed eyes. After all, it was Hannah who benefited the most. The painful subject of her past was buried now and she was free of the claims of partnership. Her grief at Naomi's death seemed genuine, but perhaps it was crocodile grief.

"We haven't really considered Don," Claudia said, tapping her pen on her pad of paper. Where I had doodles, she had organized columns of notes. She approached this as she did her writing research, with fact gathering and logical thought. I hoped, when Drake finally got hold of us and turned us over to the San Francisco police, that he would be impressed with our industry.

"What's to consider?" Bridget didn't really like suspecting anyone.

I understood. I too felt that Kim and Don were nice young folks who were ineligible as suspects. I preferred to pin the blame on Hannah because she was not a nice young person. But nice young people had committed murder before. I had even known a couple of them.

"Don doesn't seem to have any reason to have killed Naomi, or any connection aside from being the tour photographer." Bridget took the fruit knife from Hannah and cut up her own apple, with peel on. She nibbled a quarter. "He was just along for the ride, right?"

"That's not really true." Hannah looked around the table. "Don was Naomi's son, actually."

Claudia dropped her pen. Bridget blinked. I stopped doodling.

"I thought you said she wasn't married," Bridget finally said.

"She wasn't." Hannah shrugged. "We all have our indiscretions. That was Naomi's. She had a torrid affair with a married man, but he went back to his wife. When she found out she was pregnant, he gave her money for an abortion. She used the money to buy commercial baking equipment and gave the baby up for adoption. I think at the time she wanted to punish the man; if he didn't want children out of wedlock, she'd make sure he had one. But he never came around again to be punished, and she didn't enjoy the experience of childbirth at all."

"Does Don know?" Claudia leaned forward.

"I don't know." Hannah considered this. "Naomi was the one who tracked him down. She seemed to feel that since she never married and had legitimate children, she might as well get the benefit of the one she did have. He hadn't been searching for her, but she got a private detective to search for him. She told me she wanted to meet him and see what he was like before she revealed herself as his birth mother. When she found out he was a photographer, she insisted I hire him for this tour. His samples looked fine, so I hired him."

"But you don't know if Naomi told him she was his mother or not?" Bridget frowned. "I should think if she'd told him, you would all know."

"Don isn't too demonstrative." I tried to remember everything about the lanky photographer. "He might not have reacted on the surface."

"But if he thought that his rightful mother had abandoned him, and if his childhood hadn't been happy, he might have felt a lot of rage," Claudia said. Her enthusiasm for this scenario glowed in her eyes. "He might have thought she had no claim to him or his affections. He might have wanted to stop any plans she had for trying to get into his life."

"I don't know." None of these scenarios seemed right to me. "I've met both Don and Kim, and neither one seems likely to act this way. I mean, I'm not saying they wouldn't kill if pushed to it. But Naomi wasn't really pushing either of them. She was pushing Hannah."

We all turned to Hannah.

"It wasn't me, truly." Her voice squeaked. "I wouldn't have killed her. She was important to me. We haven't always gotten along, but we've always managed to work together."

Bridget glanced at the clock. I knew she didn't want this murderous coffee klatch to continue much longer; she had children to see to.

I jumped up. "I'm calling Drake." I didn't add, "Again." No need for them to know I'd snuck around behind their backs. "He's worrying about me, and I'm sitting here getting absolutely nothing done."

"You can't do that." Hannah put a hand to her throat. "We had a deal."

"You don't understand." I stood in the kitchen doorway, trying to put words to my emotions without revealing too much. "Drake is more than a policeman, see. He's my neighbor. He's a friend."

"He's going to wring your neck," Claudia said warningly. "He'll be really angry, Liz."

"Well, he has reason to be." I looked at them, sitting around the table as innocently as if we were just getting together to play cards. "Don't you see? We don't have the resources to solve this. The police know how she died, which is more than we do."

"Not necessarily," Claudia argued. "It seems to take them forever to get the lab reports back when any kind of drug or poison is involved. They may be as clueless as we are."

"But they have the scene. They know Don's and Kim's movements."

"We reconstructed that." Claudia was into her argument now. "You told us where you were, where Kim was, where everyone was except Don, and we assume he was sleeping."

"Yes, but we haven't questioned them. We haven't seen any inconsistencies in their stories. We haven't fit those together with what Hannah has to say." I shook my head. "We just don't have the big picture. I'm calling Drake."

"You don't have to," Bridget said.

"Yes, I do. It's a matter of playing fair."

"No, you don't have to." She was looking over my shoulder. With a frisson of doom, I turned too.

Drake stood in the front hall. He had one hand behind him, and I knew he was gripping the gun he kept in his waistband. Bruno Morales, his partner, stood behind him and to one side.

"Drake." I stepped out of the door, so he could see into the kitchen, where the harmless-looking group of women sat around the table. "I'm so glad you're here."

"Right." He didn't look at me after the first searing glance. "Where's the suspect?"

"You mean Hannah? She's having tea."

Bruno shook his head. "You are incredible, you women. We search the whole Peninsula for you, and all the time, you're having tea."

"Drake—"

"Later, Liz." He strode into the kitchen. "Ms. Couch? I'm going to have to ask you to come with me."

She stood slowly, throwing a reproachful look at me. I felt bad too, as if I'd turned in my best friend.

"Look, Hannah, if you're right and you didn't do it, they'll figure that out. Truly. I used to think they didn't try, but they will get to the truth."

I was babbling. Bridget came over to stand by me and put her arm around my shoulders. "It's not your fault, Liz. This was bound to happen."

"I know." I whispered to her, "I called Drake earlier. When I hid the gun."

"Oh."

"I didn't want this to be occupying your house. I didn't want the kids involved."

"I know. Thanks." She hugged me again. "And speaking of the gun—"

"Gun?" Drake whirled, his hand going to his weapon again.

"The gun Hannah used to—" With her eyes on me, I couldn't say that she abducted me. No doubt that was a horrible federal crime of some kind. "To persuade me to drive her."

"Where is it?"

"I'll get it—"

146

"Just tell Bruno."

"It's in the top filing drawer in the office. The key is on the top of that tall bookcase. I used a chair." I didn't want to be babbling so incessantly, but I couldn't make my mouth stop.

Drake's expression was so closed, so cold. I had just gotten a little used to our relationship, to the warmth and closeness we'd built together. I wasn't sure what rejection would do to me at this point, but it wouldn't be pretty.

Bruno came back in the room with the Ziploc bag containing Hannah's little gun. "It was fired, Paolo."

Drake looked at all of us. Claudia had come to stand in the kitchen door, her notebook clutched in her hand, her face mutinous. "Would anyone care to explain how this weapon came to be fired recently?"

"It went off accidentally, when Hannah was deciding to disarm." Claudia spoke before anyone else could. It looked like we were going to have womanly solidarity in the face of all this male dominance.

"No one was hurt?" Bruno looked alarmed for a moment. "The children, they are not here?"

"They're at play groups for the afternoon." Bridget spoke to Bruno. Even she was getting a little miffed with Drake's hard-ass stance.

"All right. We'll be back sometime later to take statements from the rest of you."

"Bridget could follow us to the station and give her statement before picking up her children at their play groups," Bruno murmured. "Then we would not need to disrupt her evening."

I could see that Drake cared little about disrupting anyone's evening, but he nodded curt agreement, his hand on Hannah's arm. "Let's go, Ms. Couch." He gestured at me with his head. "You too, Liz."

Bridget walked with me to the police cruiser, and gave me one last squeeze. "It'll be okay. You'll see."

But she was worried. And so was I.

15_____

I had been in the little interview room at the Palo Alto police station before, a few years ago. I hadn't known Drake then; he'd been just another police officer trying to move me along. At the time I lived in my VW bus on the streets of Palo Alto, and tried to have as little contact as possible with the powers that be. If anyone had told me then that I'd not only be neighborly with a policeman, but something far more intimate, I would have thought that person was crazy.

Now I wondered if I was crazy. Drake had been assuring me for the past year that a relationship was possible between us, despite the wide divergence in our lifestyles. Not that I wanted my lifestyle to involve murder and its aftermath. But it happened. And every time, I felt cut off from him, by his policemanly attitude toward my behavior. I try to behave well. I follow my own moral code, which holds me to a much higher standard than most of the people in government making the rules we all have to live by. But when push comes to shove, I'm still on one side of the fence, the outlaw side, with Drake on the other.

And given the way he was acting, no one would be opening the gate anytime soon.

He and Bruno were questioning Hannah in a different room. Bruno had told me that much, when I'd asked what the drill was. Drake wouldn't talk to me at all. He had driven the police cruiser to city hall while Bruno sat sideways in his seat, chatting amiably. They would let the San Francisco police department know we had been located. Depending on how it went, they would take us up there, or the San Francisco police would come down to fetch us.

"I don't see why you need Liz," Hannah had said, looking down her nose as she was so good at doing. "She was just doing her job, obeying my orders."

"She will be involved in the questioning," Bruno said. He spoke mildly, but with finality.

Bruno had taken my statement after Hannah had been led off. Now I waited. And I began to get angry. I expected that the San Francisco police would treat me as a criminal, because they knew nothing about me except that I had a prior conviction.

But Drake should have known better. I had done my best. I had kept myself and anyone else from getting killed. I had called him as soon as possible. Why, then, was he so upset that he couldn't even look at me, much less say an encouraging word?

I wore no watch, but I estimated it to be close to four P.M. One of the longest days of my life was still in progress, with no end in sight. I sighed, and pictured Barker. He was probably sitting, with his leash in his mouth, on the rug in front of the door, staring at it, willing it to open and reveal me or my substitute. Something told me that I wasn't going to be free to walk him for at least a few more hours.

Finally the door opened and Bruno came in. He sat on the other side of the table and looked at me sadly.

"I am sorry, Liz. This is not really fair. But the San Francisco police wish us to take you up to the hotel, where they are still investigating. They question your story, you see."

"They can question it all they like, but it's the truth. Doesn't Hannah corroborate it?"

"She has contacted her lawyer, and he has advised her to say nothing until he arranges for a suitable attorney to be there, which could be as long as tomorrow. The police are very frustrated with this, naturally, and they wish to take you through your account at the scene. It seems that they have heard you slapped the deceased yesterday."

"She slapped me first." As soon as I said it, I thought how childish it sounded. "Is Bridget still here?"

"She has given her statement and gone to pick up her children." Bruno tapped his fingers on the table. "For what it's worth, her statement corroborates yours."

"Great." I could see his watch, upside down on his wrist. It was three-forty. Barker would be good for another two or three hours at most. "Let's get it over with. Sooner or later they'll figure out who really did this, and then I can go about my business."

Bruno hesitated. "If you will promise not to try to escape, I will not arrest you. However, the San Francisco police may do so. Once we are up there, they may hold you without charging you, at least until Ms. Couch talks. Do you understand?"

"Sure," I said, acting nonchalant.

I was struggling with tears, actually. My feelings were hurt that Bruno, who I'd come to count a friend, was treating me like this, even though I knew that he had to. I took a deep breath, then another.

"You have the right to remain silent," Bruno droned. "Anything you say can and will be used against you in a court of law. You have the right to speak to an attorney. You can have an attorney present. If you cannot afford an attorney, one will be provided without charge. You have the right to one phone call."

"I don't care about a lawyer or any of that nonsense. I want to call Bridget and ask her to take care of Barker for me."

"She said to tell you that she will care for your dog." Bruno looked troubled. "You should call an attorney, Liz. My wife knows someone who will represent you without charging too much."

"Anything is too much. I don't need an attorney. I haven't done anything wrong."

The door opened before he could answer me. Drake stood there. His face was set in those hard lines I wasn't used to seeing. He still wouldn't look directly at me.

"Are you ready? Let's go," he said to Bruno.

Bruno hesitated. "Perhaps you should stay here, Paolo. There is no necessity for us both to go."

"If either of them gets away, we'll never hear the end of it."

I opened my mouth, then shut it again. There was no point talking to someone who wouldn't look at you. A part of me that Drake had gradually coaxed into warmth and friendship began to shrivel.

Bruno looked from me to Drake. "Liz will not flee. She has promised."

"Let's go. I don't want Scarlatti and the rest of those

city cops talking behind my back. If they have anything to say, they can say it to my face."

This was a bewildering statement. While Drake strode on ahead, gripping Hannah's arm firmly enough to draw a protest from her, I whispered to Bruno, "What was that about? Why would they talk behind his back?"

"As you are asking me to do?" Bruno shook his head, then relented. "Because a woman who was presumed to be abducted used Paolo's telephone to call her attorney, who gave that number to the police in Massachusetts, who passed it along to San Francisco. We were obliged to search both your house and Paolo's house to make sure you were not there." Bruno hesitated. "He was worried, Liz. He was afraid he would find your body."

I stole a look at Drake's unyielding back, marching down the hall. "Well, thank goodness I managed not to be killed. He appears so grateful for that."

"Give it time," Bruno urged. "He will settle. Of course it looks bad that a suspect in an abduction has a key to his house. That is why he goes to San Francisco too, because he wants to confront that issue."

"So now I've ruined his job. I knew this relationship was a mistake." I took another deep breath. I never used to cry, no matter how bad things got. I would not start now. There would be plenty of time for that later.

"No, no." Bruno said no more, because we were at the elevator to the parking garage, but he patted my hand. Drake stood facing the doors. He hustled Hannah out of the elevator and into the backseat of an unmarked car. Bruno hopped in with her.

"What are you doing?" Drake spoke to him in a furious undertone. "Suspects in the back."

"In case she tries to leap from the car, you understand." Bruno turned his limpid gaze on Drake. "I must be ready, Paolo. Of course Liz will not try that. She may sit up front with you."

"I'll keep Hannah from jumping out," I said. The knot of emotion that clogged my throat made it difficult to speak.

"I'm not going to jump out." Hannah sniffed. "Let's go. I want my attorney; I want this to be over."

"We all do." Drake's pinched features didn't relax when he spoke. "Bruno, let's get going. The traffic will be bad enough already."

Bruno fastened his seat belt in the backseat. "Climb in, Liz," he said, smiling at me.

I didn't want to drive up to the City in thick traffic beside a man who radiated anger at me. But it seemed I had no choice.

The last time a man evinced such harsh emotions in my direction, I'd ended up in jail. This time, I was sure that after all the stories had been told, after Bridget's statement had been read by the San Francisco police, I would be free. But the tentative blossoming of feelings between myself and Paul Drake, I feared, was irreparably damaged.

He chose to go up 280, hoping to duck some of the traffic. I sat passively in the front seat, not moving, not talking, as if maintaining a low profile would get me out of trouble. It had worked in the past. I didn't think it would this time.

In the backseat, Bruno chatted amiably with Hannah about the renovation he and his wife Lucy were doing. Everyone was renovating. Everyone wanted bigger houses. The face of Palo Alto was changing. More than ever, it was becoming an enclave of the rich.

154

I felt sad about that. I had planned to live the rest of my life in my little cottage, fixing only what was necessary to keep it standing. But if I had to sell to escape the bad vibes coming from the house in front of me, at least I'd get top dollar.

I would be able to afford a place in Denver, close to my folks. The notion was not a happy one. My family was not especially rich in warmth, and my parents made a lot of judgments about me that I found painful to live with. But it seemed preferable to enduring the feelings Drake was dishing out.

At this point in my brooding, I detected an unfortunate pattern. After serving time for trying to kill my abusive husband, I'd begun running away, spurred on by his attempts to find and punish me. By the time I'd confronted him, it had almost been too late to salvage my self-respect. Now I was planning how to run away from another man, one fundamentally decent and caring.

I wanted to put my head down on my knees and weep. And I wanted to scream at Drake. It had been his insistence that had made me open up, caused me to unwrap my vulnerabilities.

By the time we reached South San Francisco, my thoughts had shifted from my present misery to trying to imagine a future without Drake. If he cut himself off from me, which might well happen if his job was on the line over our association, what would I do? I had become dependent on him, and that didn't sit well with me. I used his telephone instead of getting one of my own. When my ancient computer faltered, he figured out the reason. I had been in a time warp after three years of living in my bus, with no access to media except the magazines that bought my articles. He had brought me up to date on current events, introduced me to movies, made me reevaluate my loner stance.

I opened my knapsack and got my notebook out. Ignoring the notes we'd made about Naomi's death, I turned to a fresh page. It looked like I wouldn't need to worry about how Naomi met her end. The police would do that in their usual clear-cutting fashion, hacking down the forest to get to the one guilty tree.

"What are you doing?" Drake's voice was flat, devoid of emotion. It was the first time he'd spoken to me on the whole trip.

"I'm figuring out how much more I need to earn each month to afford a telephone."

His mouth tightened. He took a right where Highway 1 turned into Nineteenth Avenue, and we drove along Junipero Serra in silence for a few minutes. The traffic was thick, but Drake moved through it with automatic ease.

"If you'd done that when I first asked you to," he said finally, spitting out the words as if they caused him pain, "none of this would have happened."

"That's a crock and you know it, mate." The casual endearment slipped out without my realizing it. We had called each other that, in fake Australian accents, at some of our tenderest moments. I rushed to fill the small, pregnant silence between us. "Of course, your career wouldn't have been endangered by my illicit use of your phone, but everything else would still have happened."

"If you'd had a real job—"

"This was a real job. The kind in an office, like you are always after me to get. Keyboarding, answering the phones, filing. It lasted for all of five hours. I'm realist enough to know that something in me is not acceptable in an office setting, even if you still think all I need is a pair of pantyhose and a meek demeanor."

The chitchat in the backseat ceased. Drake didn't reply, and I felt ashamed of my outburst—but not very. What I said was the truth, no matter how unpalatable it was to him. I had temped in many offices, and I had never been asked back after my initial assignment was over. Not because I was inefficient. I worked steadily and didn't steal office supplies or make personal telephone calls. But somehow I didn't fit in with the other cubicle dwellers.

I could understand why Drake wanted me to have a real job. I would have health insurance, retirement, the safety net that was so important. And I had come to want those things too. If I got sick, if I had a serious accident, I would be in trouble.

At least I had come to terms with my inability to do the corporate culture thing. And I knew that if trouble was looking for a person, it would find them, whether they worked at home or in an office.

"I'm sorry if I'm being mean," I said, low voiced. In the backseat, Bruno had resumed his light chat with Hannah Couch; he was a model of thoughtfulness. "I know it's a setback to your career to be associated with a person like me. I've known it all along. We can call it quits right now. No questions asked."

He didn't reply for a moment. Then he pulled the car over two lanes of traffic and turned into a convenience store parking lot.

"Paolo?" Bruno sounded startled.

"Liz needs to use the bathroom," Drake said brusquely. He came around and opened the car door on my side. "Come on."

"I don't—"

"I said, come on." He looked formidable, not at all like the comfortable, frizzy-haired companion I was used to. I got out of the car slowly. In the back of my mind are always alarm bells associated with overbearing masculine behavior. I was pretty sure he wouldn't hit me, but with men you can't always tell.

"We have to buy something," I said. I had a lot of experience with public bathrooms, after my years of living in my bus. "Otherwise they won't let you use the bathroom."

He led me into the store, past the bored clerk, who chatted with a bored customer. We stood in the hall that led to the rest rooms.

"There's no privacy to talk about this now," he said, still tight lipped. "But you are not getting out of our relationship so easily. You are not running from me. We will have this out when the investigation is finished, but I have no intention of letting you blame this on me being concerned about my career. What I'm concerned about, damn it, is you." His hands closed over my shoulders and he shook me, though with more restraint than I expected, considering the way he looked at me. "You driving around with a woman who has a gun on you. You being Miss Hero and helping that idiot Claudia take the gun away. You jumping in to try and clear this crazy Hannah Couch from the murder charge she no doubt richly deserves. You putting your life at risk."

I thought he would shake me again, but instead he pulled me close and held me for the space of several heartbeats.

"You put your life at risk every day." My voice was muffled by his chest. I pulled away, and let some of my own anger loose. "You nag me about my job, but you have the most dangerous one possible. Who the hell do you think you are, Paul Drake? What gives you the right to tell me what I can and can't do? When do I do that to you?"

His hands dropped. "You don't," he said, rubbing his face. "I've wondered why. Guess you don't care as much as I do."

He turned, but I grabbed his arm and pulled him back around to face me. "That's bunk too. I don't show my love by trying to run your life. I may hate the risk your job involves, but it doesn't change my feelings for you. For all the good they do me."

He stared down at me, his face blank, his glasses reflecting the light. "You don't show your love," he said slowly. "I certainly realize that. Trying to pry emotion out of you is like interrogating the mute. But you—you feel—love? For me?"

I reached up and took his glasses off so I could see his eyes. They blazed with such brightness I couldn't bear to look. It was like facing the sun.

"I do," I said.

He kissed me. I kissed him back. It was the best embrace of my life. All the troubles fell away in a magical combination of tenderness and heat.

The counter person coughed ostentatiously, and Drake tore his lips away. I gazed at him, bemused, and realized I still had his glasses dangling from my limp fingers. I put them back on, adjusting them as best I could.

He pushed them up his nose and stared at me with laser intentness. "Marry me."

It wasn't the first time he'd proposed, but I had managed

to treat the previous occasions as banter, and he hadn't pursued them. This time it was different.

"No."

He pulled me close again. "Damn it, why not? I need to have that tie, Liz. I need you to be in my life on a permanent basis."

"This isn't the time to talk about it." I could see down the aisle of chips to the front window. "Bruno is alone with Hannah. What if she tries to run away?"

"He'll have to stop her." Drake put his cheek on top of my head. It made me ache for what I was afraid we could never have.

"Like you said, mate. When this is over, we'll have that talk. We'll put our cards on the table. I'll see your point of view, you'll see mine. Until then—"

He held me a little away. "It would help you with the San Francisco police if I said you were my fiancée."

"That's the worst reason to get engaged I ever heard." I pushed him away altogether. "I sure hope your romantic proposal in aisle six wasn't motivated by this."

He started to smile, for the first time that day. "Guess you'll have to wait and see."

I started back toward the door. "Look, let's get this over. The sooner everything is wrapped up, the sooner I can take your generous offer apart for you."

He took my arm. "Stop trying to take the lead here. You're still in protective custody. And when you consider my offer, remember that it comes with lots of extras, like health and dental insurance. Costco membership."

"Death benefits?" I shook my head. "I don't aspire to be a policeman's wife, or a policeman's widow, come to that."

"I don't aspire to be a corpse," he retorted.

The clerk watched us go out the door. We hadn't bought the obligatory soda or chips. But she didn't say anything. She was probably just happy to have the crazy people leave.

16

THE jackals of the press were in command of the hotel's entrance and lobby. We went up to the suite in the freight elevator, like a rewind of our trip down earlier— was it really the same day? So much had happened since Hannah had comandeered me with a gun under her raincoat. I glanced at her as we rode in the clanking elevator car. She looked stern, remote, unflappable. Even when she lost her head, she kept her wits about her.

The kitchen door was locked. Drake rang the service bell, and after a moment a uniformed cop answered it.

"Drake. Palo Alto police."

"Right." The uniform stepped aside. Her nameplate said DIAZ. "Watch where you walk. We've had the crime-scene people in here for the last few hours, and they've left a mess."

The doors to Kim's and Don's bedrooms were closed. When we entered the little kitchen, we saw what the cop meant about the mess. Every cupboard stood open. The bins of staples that Hannah had brought with her were opened as well, and their contents strewn throughout the room.

Something crunched underfoot. I looked down to see broken bits of rainbow-colored glass.

Hannah's expression had grown more forbidding. When she saw the broken glass, she stopped.

"My carnival-glass bowl! How did that get broken?"

Officer Diaz shrugged. She looked sympathetic. "These things happen. The crime-scene technicians vacuum up everything, then the evidence people search. It would be tidier if it was the other way around, but that wouldn't work."

Hannah bent to pick up one of the pieces, and Officer Diaz put a hand on her arm. "Please don't touch anything. When we're through, you can do that. If you're still around."

"What do you mean? Why wouldn't I be around?"

Officer Diaz didn't answer. She opened the door into the suite's main room, and we filed in.

The area around the couches and coffee table was cordoned off with yellow tape. Here again, the contents of closets and drawers had been pulled out and rummaged through.

"The inspectors are over there." Officer Diaz pointed to the library alcove at one side of the room. Two people, a man and a woman, were bent over something on the large, polished wood desk.

I was watching them, so I didn't see Kim until she jumped up from the chair she'd pulled around to face the floor-to-ceiling balcony windows.

"Liz! Hannah! You're back!" She ran to me, and I hugged her. She was trembling.

"I was afraid," she whispered to me. "Afraid something awful had happened to you."

"Well, I had to take Hannah shopping at the second-hand store. That was pretty awful."

She laughed, a little hysterically, and stepped back.

"Hannah, I'm glad you're safe." Her voice quavered. "It's been terrible here."

"Kim, my dear." Hannah sounded sincere. "I left you holding the bag. I'm so sorry."

Kim looked surprised at this display of compassion. "We didn't know what to do. It was—difficult."

"I'm sure it must have been." Hannah looked around the room. "Where's Don?"

"He's in his room. They said we could stay in our rooms if we liked, after they searched them." Kim shivered. "I didn't want to be alone. I've just been . . . staring out the window." Her voice fell. "I'm so sorry."

"I'm sorry too." Hannah actually hugged Kim. "Naomi was your aunt, after all. You must miss her."

Kim darted a look at the two inspectors, who had come forward during this exchange. "I haven't had time yet to know how I feel," she said honestly. "All I can think about is that awful moment when she fell—" She put a hand to her mouth and looked at us, her eyes huge.

"It wasn't particularly nice," Hannah agreed with massive understatement.

"I'm Inspector Scarlatti, and this is Inspector Daly," said the woman, offering her hand. "May I say what a pleasure it is to meet you, Ms. Couch? I'm a fan of yours."

Hannah shook the offered hand, smiling graciously. "Thank you."

The inspector's smile cooled a lot when she turned to me. She didn't offer her hand. "Ms. Sullivan."

"Inspector."

"We've looked over your statement, Ms. Sullivan," Inspector Daly broke in. "In light of your previous record, we'd like to ask you more questions."

Hannah frowned. "Did my attorney show up?"

"Not yet." Scarlatti shook her head.

"Well," Hannah said, "I don't know when he'll get here, but I'm prepared to make a statement about my movements after the—after Naomi died."

"In good time," Daly said, concentrating on me.

"Young man, what I have to say will make it unnecessary for you to spend a lot of time on Liz." Hannah drew herself up. "I'm prepared to take full responsibility—"

"Oh, no," Kim broke in. "No, no, no." Her voice rose hysterically. "You didn't kill her. Did you?"

The inspectors exchanged glances with Officer Diaz, who went to Kim. "I think you'd be happier in your room, Ms. Matthews."

"I don't want to be in there alone!" Kim was capable of putting out some decibels when she tried.

"I'll stay with you." Officer Diaz led Kim through the kitchen. We could hear their feet crunching.

Inspector Scarlatti turned back to us. "Ms. Couch, why don't you go with Inspector Daly? He'll take your statement. I'll speak with Ms. Sullivan." She looked at Drake and Bruno. "Did you two want to stay around?" Her smile turned teasing. She was a good-looking woman, not much older than I, with straight blond hair and no wedding ring. "See how it's done in the big city?"

"Sure thing, Bianca." Drake smiled back at her. I could see that, though she was a couple of inches taller than he was, she thought he was cute. It made me feel rather smug. "We always benefit from watching the pros, right, Bruno?"

Bruno nodded. "We don't have many capital cases in our area. You are sure to solve this very complicated matter quickly, is that not so?"

Bianca Scarlatti's expression turned speculative. "From what I can tell, Ms. Sullivan has been involved in several of your recent murder cases. How do you explain that?"

"Can we sit down?" Drake broke in quickly. "It's been a long day."

"Of course." Scarlatti led us over to the sofas grouped in front of the fireplace. Inspector Daly had already taken Hannah off to the library alcove. We could hear the low murmur of his voice, her stringent tone when she answered, but we couldn't discern the words.

"I thought you wanted to know about what happened today." I settled myself, and wished that I had taken Bruno up on his offer of an attorney. "What does that have to do with the past?"

"You have a history of being involved in murder cases." Scarlatti made her voice patient. "Why is that?"

"Well, because Detective Drake is my neighbor, I guess."

She shot Drake a skeptical look. He sat at his ease, one arm stretched out along the back of the sofa, one foot hiked up on the opposite knee, but I could see the lines of tension around his mouth.

"Well, Detective?"

He shrugged. "She's my neighbor. I don't invite her into my cases, but she does sometimes become involved inadvertently. All those murders have been satisfactorily resolved, and no suspicion attaches to her."

"In a couple of cases," Bruno put in, "she has been instrumental in finding the solution. Is that not right, Paolo?"

Drake scowled at me. "I don't approve of civilians helping to investigate. Liz knows that. But it's true that she is a good observer, and capable of deduction."

"Very impressive." Scarlatti sounded sarcastic. "But Ms. Sullivan is an ex-con."

"You know, I can speak for myself," I said when Drake opened his mouth. He shut up.

I turned to Scarlatti. "This is an old story, one I'm tired of telling. My husband beat me, and I was fool enough to think each time was the last time. The actual last time, I thought he was going to kill me. I managed to get the gun before he did, and I shot him. He didn't die. I went to jail, and I divorced him, and even though he kept stalking me, I'm glad now that I wasn't the person who finally ended up killing him, because I don't want to be a killer. I don't like violence. I don't approve of murder. I'm no vigilante; I don't see myself as ridding the world of murderers or anything of that nature. I've been through a lot of awful stuff, and I just want a peaceful life. Does that answer your questions?"

Scarlatti tapped a pencil against her lips. "If you don't like violence, how do you explain slapping the deceased yesterday?"

"If Kim told you that story, she undoubtedly told you all of it. Naomi slapped me. It seemed to me that she was used to getting away with bullying people. I slapped her back. It wasn't really a considered decision, but I don't regret it. She deserved it."

Scarlatti made a note. "So how did you come to hook up with Hannah Couch?"

"I do temp work, and a media relations firm hired me to type and file. This job came in as an emergency, and there was no one to drive but the owner, Judi Kershay. She asked me to do it. She offered me a lot of money. I accepted."

"Why didn't Judi Kershay drive?" Scarlatti pounced on this tidbit.

I shrugged. "She has some kind of history with Hannah. As it turns out, no one wants to drive Hannah, because she's capricious and demanding, and Naomi was worse. She had summarily fired the people who'd set up the tour, and her publishers begged Judi to take it on as a favor. At least, that's what Judi told me. Maybe you should talk to her."

"Thanks for the advice," Scarlatti said. "Maybe we will." She got to her feet, a tall, graceful blonde, and walked over to the windows, pulling a cell phone out of her bag.

"She hasn't mellowed," Bruno said to Paul in a low voice.

"She's full of herself," he agreed, "but she does good work. We just might be here awhile."

"You don't have to stay on my account." I tried to sound independent, instead of forlorn. "I can get the train back."

"We're concerned in the investigation," Bruno told me gently. "She will start to rake us over the coals soon. We can't leave until then."

"So they obviously don't think Naomi died of a heart attack, if they're going to all this trouble."

"I'd say they have a pretty good idea of how she died, even without the toxicology tests." Drake's fingers tapped impatiently on the back of the couch.

Scarlatti returned, holstering her cell phone. "Now. Why don't you give me the story about this morning, Ms. Sullivan?"

I went through it for her, how I'd driven up from Palo

Alto, the tension when I arrived, the confrontation that had ended with Naomi's death.

Scarlatti wrote it down, though she was taping me too. I didn't know if she believed me. Since Hannah was evidently willing to say that she'd done the abducting, I thought we might get out of there quickly after all.

"As you're such a good observer," Scarlatti said when I finished telling her about the morning, "is there anything else you noticed while you were working with Ms. Couch and Ms. Matthews the previous day?" She darted a mischievous look at Drake and Bruno. "Remember, these guys were bragging about you."

"Thanks for putting me on the spot," I said to Drake. "Actually, some weird things happened yesterday." I told Scarlatti about the notes that had frightened Hannah, and the arrangement of forget-me-nots and ivy she had commanded me to throw away. About the quarrel over the crepe maker, and Naomi's drinking at the FanciFoods event. I told her everything I could think of that might give her an idea. I didn't tell her anything Hannah had told us around Bridget's table. I was going to let Hannah tell about finding and destroying Naomi's tell-all manuscript. And it seemed to me that someone should tell Don that he was Naomi's son before the police found out about it, though I wasn't sure how that could be accomplished. And perhaps he already knew. Perhaps he'd known before the whole thing had started.

"You are a good observer, if you're not making this up." Scarlatti put down her pen and stared at me speculatively.

"Kim was there when I threw away the flowers. She even said someone gave Hannah a similar arrangement when they left Boston. And Kim was at the TV station when Hannah implied that Naomi did away with her brother, who was Kim's uncle. Didn't she tell you about this stuff?"

"She's been less than coherent, and the other one, Don, hardly says two words." Scarlatti got to her feet. "I'm going to bring them all over here, in the interests of brevity, and see if we can get some agreement."

Before she could do so, the front door of the suite opened. Another uniformed cop escorted a tall, well-dressed man into the room. "Attorney for Hannah Couch," the uniform announced, and then let himself back out.

Hannah walked around the library desk. "I'm so glad you came," she said, doing her gracious act, holding out her hand.

The man took it. "Richard Kendall. Nice to meet you, Ms. Couch." He looked at the police with haughty determination. "We need a private room so I can confer with my client."

"You can use one of these bedrooms," Scarlatti said, heading toward the kitchen. "We're going to ask Don and Kim to come in for a while."

I caught Hannah's arm as she went by. "Don't you think someone should tell Don . . . ?"

Hannah paused, taken aback. "Well, I don't want to. It's not really my place."

"Tell him what?" Scarlatti thrust herself between us.

"My client has nothing more to say until I've had a chance to speak with her," Richard Kendall said with authority.

"It's nothing to do with this." Hannah shook off Kendall, returning to her more usual brusque manner. "Don, you know, was adopted. He's actually Naomi's son. She gave him up at birth. A couple of months ago she had private detectives search for him, and she asked me to hire him for this tour. That's all I know. Maybe she already told him. In any case, I can't do it."

She turned back to Kendall. "What are we waiting for?" Still regal, she led him through the kitchen, crunching debris as they went.

Scarlatti looked a little dazed. "You get used to it," I said to her kindly.

"How did you know this?"

"After Hannah kidnapped me, she also abducted a friend who stopped by my house when she saw news reports that I was a dangerous criminal."

"We faxed you the statement Bridget Montrose made," Drake added. "I assume you've looked at it. It substantiates Ms. Sullivan's statement."

"I've looked at it." Scarlatti didn't say anything else.

I looked narrowly at her. "Perhaps I should have a word with Mr. Kendall when he's finished being run through Hannah's wringer. The loss of the good name I've been trying to build up for the past few years could be worth something."

Scarlatti waved that away and towed me back to the sofa. "Go on. Hannah abducted you, then your friend."

"She made us take her to the thrift store to shop for vintage linens."

"Oh, the horror!" Scarlatti rolled her eyes.

"Well, being held at gunpoint and made to look for linens isn't the worst thing that ever happened to me, but it's on the list. Anyway, after that she wanted to go to Bridget's house—my friend—because she thought they might be staking out my house. So while we were sitting around at Bridget's, we offered to try and figure out the crime so she would let us go." I came to a halt. "It sounds

171

lame, but we didn't have a lot of options until after we'd disarmed her."

"At that point you didn't call 911," Scarlatti mentioned.

"I did call Drake. Bridget had promised not to call the police. I didn't promise. Anyway, while we were hashing through it, Hannah mentioned this about Don."

"Anything else you're holding back?"

"I'm not holding it back," I said, irritated. "I just feel someone should tell Don in a decent way that Naomi was his mother."

"You're right. Someone should." Don spoke from behind me. We turned to see Don and Kim in the kitchen doorway, with Officer Diaz behind them. Kim had her hand to her mouth. Don was impassive, but he started blinking. He pulled one of the chairs out from the big table and sat abruptly, burying his head in his hands.

Kim patted him on the shoulder. "Don, I'm so sorry." She looked at us. "He lost his mom—I guess his adoptive mom—last year. Maybe he and Naomi could have—" Her eyes filled with tears. "Oh, it's all so awful."

The front door opened again. "Ms. Kershay." The officer appeared to be getting into his role as hotel butler. He almost bowed as he ushered Judi Kershay into the room.

Judi looked around at all of us, her gaze fixing on me. "Liz, are you okay? I've been so worried about you after the reports came out. I tried to call you on the cell phone, but you didn't answer."

"Hannah turned off all the cell phones."

"You thought Liz was the one to worry about?" Inspector Daly posed the question smoothly. "Not Ms. Couch?"

"Never Hannah." Judi looked from him to Scarlatti,

evidently pegging them as the authorities. "I knew Hannah was behind it as soon as I heard the report on the radio."

"But you didn't call to correct us," Scarlatti said. "I wonder why?"

"We all wonder why," Drake put in. "It would have been nice for Liz if the media had stopped branding her as an abductor. Why didn't you say anything?"

Judi looked bewildered. "I did call the hotel and asked to be put in touch with whoever was investigating. I was put on hold, and then a voice mail said to leave a message, so I did. No one got back to me until half an hour ago. I thought you were calling me back. Who are all you people, and why should I answer anything? Am I under suspicion? Do I need an attorney?"

"There's one in the other room, but Hannah has him sewn up." I had an insane urge to babble. The tension in the room was getting thick, and my impulse was to try and dissipate it. "Maybe he has friends we can talk to."

"You are not currently at risk of being charged," Scarlatti said, sending me a quelling look before turning to Judi. "If you're afraid anything you say could incriminate you, you should have an attorney present."

"Well, it couldn't incriminate me. It goes back to a promise I made Hannah the last time I drove for her."

"We're waiting." Scarlatti gestured Judi into one of the chairs around the fireplace. I didn't know why she didn't take her aside, but perhaps she didn't think it would be any big thing.

Judi was hesitant. "I said I would never tell anyone."

"You can tell us."

"All of you?"

"Just spill it, Ms. Kershay." Scarlatti was impatient.

"Well . . ." Judi thought for a moment. "If you say so. Hannah uses cake mixes."

17

"**THAT'S** it?" Scarlatti looked puzzled. "That's your big secret? That Hannah uses cake mix?"

"It's not possible," Kim squeaked. She turned away from Don to stare at Judi. "She would never, never . . . everything is made from scratch. Everything."

"That's what you're supposed to believe. But the last tour I did for her, for *Hannah Does Desserts*, her food stylist quit in a huff, and Naomi wasn't feeling well, which I took to be a euphemism for hung over. Hannah had to turn out a lot of lemon pound cake for a book event and demonstration at the Home Chef; they'd sold tickets, and everyone was expecting dessert. I walked into the kitchen in this very suite, and caught her with the mix boxes."

"She would never compromise her standards," Kim insisted, close to tears. "She's always said that. Always insisted—"

"That everyone else do so." Judi nodded. "I know. She'd told me in no uncertain terms that she had to have unsalted European butter for the demonstration part of the event, and special flour from one certain mill, and free-range eggs, and organic Meyer lemons, and a certain kind of baking powder I had never heard of. I busted my butt chasing all that stuff down, and then found out she was using shortcuts in secret. I'm afraid I gloated a bit."

"Anyone would," Inspector Scarlatti said, her voice unsteady. She bit her lips. "So what did you do? Black-mail her?"

"In a way," Judi admitted. "She had a lot of complaints about my company and my employees. I said if she made her feelings known to the publisher, which was her threat, I would tell all. I wouldn't have, not really. Confidentiality is an important part of what I do. But I might have joked about it a bit in the media community, and she knew that could get around. So we agreed to a pact of mutual silence."

At my side, Drake shook with silent laughter. It was hard to imagine Hannah with cake mixes, after all her self-righteous pontificating on the correct, and time-consuming, way to do things.

Kim didn't think it was funny. "If it was an emergency," she said haltingly, "if she had to get the cakes out on a very tight schedule—but still. Couldn't people tell the difference?"

"People want to believe that a celebrity is perfect," Judi said cynically. "They say, 'Oh, this is wonderful. I've never tasted anything so good.' "

Don paid no attention to this tempest in a cake pan. He still sat by the table, staring at the intricate pattern of the oriental rug.

"Well, this is fascinating," Scarlatti said briskly, "but it doesn't get us any forwarder." She nodded at the officer who stood by the door. "Will you take Ms. Kershay downstairs and get her statement in order, get it signed? If we need you again, Ms. Kershay, we'll call you."

"Fine," Judi nodded. She caught my eye. "I might as well take the cell phone and stuff now."

I rummaged in my backpack and got out the folder, the expense money, and the cell phone. "I kind of enjoyed it for a while," I told her.

"I'm sorry for the trouble, Liz. When you're in the market for a job, call me. I think you did well under a lot of pressure."

After Judi left, there was silence for a moment. Scarlatti stared consideringly at Kim, who looked nervous at being on the receiving end of her scrutiny.

Finally the inspector said, "Liz says there have been incidents involving forget-me-nots and ivy."

Kim looked confused. "I'm not sure . . ."

"That arrangement yesterday," I prompted. "You said—"

"Please let her speak for herself," Scarlatti said, at the same time Drake dug his elbow into my ribs. I subsided. I know better than to interrupt when the police are working, but this was the strangest investigation I'd ever seen. I raised my eyebrows at Drake, and he shrugged. Evidently he was finding it incomprehensible too.

"It's true," Kim said hesitantly. "We were at the airport in Boston. This messenger came rushing up to us with a cute dish of ivy and little blue flowers, done up like florists do, you know. Naomi gave him a tip, but Hannah just got this funny look on her face and walked over to the nearest trash can and dumped it."

"Did she say anything?"

"No." Kim shook her head. "Naomi said, 'What did you do that for?' and then Hannah said, 'You know why,' or something like that. Then we got on the plane, and I'd never flown before, so I was kinda excited, and I forgot all about it until I saw Liz throwing away the same stuff yesterday."

Scarlatti walked over to the desk and used the house phone for a brief colloquy. When she hung up she said to Inspector Daly, "No luck. Someone left the order in an envelope on the gift-shop counter, with enough cash to pay for it."

"I don't get it," Kim said, her brow furrowed. "Like, everything was about Hannah, wasn't it? That note in the car that she didn't like getting. She said she was going to get it tested because whoever licked the envelope left their DNA on it. And the flowers. But Naomi was the one who died. Isn't that funny?"

"Funny isn't the word for it," Inspector Daly said.

Scarlatti held up a hand. "Back up here. Notes Hannah didn't like getting. Let's talk about those. Liz said there were a couple of them. One amongst her messages when you got to the hotel."

Kim shook her head. "I don't—"

"You didn't see that one. Okay. Tell us about the one you did see."

"It was on the seat of the car after we did the TV thing last night." Kim looked troubled. "Really, that's all I know. I thought maybe it was fan mail, and Hannah would like that and stop—"

She halted. "Stop what?" Scarlatti was taking notes.

"Stop being such a pain. She and Naomi both. They were at each other's throats. Naomi was so angry about the crepe maker. I've never seen her that angry before, not even—"

This time Scarlatti waited a little longer before prompting her. "Not even when?"

Kim looked around at all of us. Her eyes filled with

178

tears. "I guess everyone knows what she said. What Hannah said. That Naomi—killed my uncle."

Don stirred. "I didn't know. Seems like there was a lot I didn't know." His voice was bitter.

"I'm sorry." Kim's tears overflowed. "I don't know why you're making me talk about this in front of everyone. I—of course, it couldn't be true. My uncle had a heart attack. Everyone knew his heart was bad. He wouldn't diet or exercise or anything the doctor told him to do. He still loved the fettuccine Alfredo with lots of cream."

"Tell me about your uncle's death." Scarlatti's voice was gentler.

"Well, okay, but it couldn't have anything to do with this. I mean, Aunt Naomi could be a real bitch sometimes, but she wouldn't—"

"Oh, right," Don said heavily, as if it had just occurred to him. "I have a cousin." He looked at Kim and his mouth quirked up for a brief moment. "At least that's something good."

Kim looked back, a smile trembling on her lips. "You have lots of cousins, and a couple more aunts and uncles. I have a big family. They'll all love you."

"More than my birth mom, evidently." Don unfolded his lanky frame from the chair and paced across the room and back. "She didn't even try to get to know me. I could feel her watching, always watching, but I figured she was waiting for me to make a mistake. I didn't know she was . . . checking me out."

"If we can get back to my question," Scarlatti said. "I want to hear about the circumstances of your uncle's death. I understand he had a big dustup with your aunt just before his heart attack."

179

"It was the day before, actually," Kim said. Her forehead creased with the effort of remembering. "He wanted to buy the business. He'd been managing it for so long, since I was little. It was always understood that at some point Naomi would sell it to him. When my aunt Mary—that's his wife—would complain he wasn't being paid enough for all his long hours and hard work, he would tell her he was building equity. I guess Naomi told him if he worked for less, she'd take that into account in the sale price."

Kim took a deep breath. Her gaze went back to Don, who stood by the balcony windows watching her. "You're not getting a good picture of my family, but really, Naomi was the meanest one." Then she caught her breath. "Not that she wasn't—I mean—"

Again that brief smile, more like a twitch of the lips. "That's okay. I can't think of her as my mother. I had a great mother, actually. Sounds like it's a good thing I was given up for adoption."

"Oh, dear." Kim started to get up.

"Ms. Matthews, please. Just finish the story." Inspector Daly looked at Scarlatti. "Maybe it would be better if we did this separately."

"I know what I'm doing, Ian." Scarlatti waved him back. "Kim, do you mind? We could take you into the other room."

"Really, I don't mind," Kim said earnestly. "I mean, I did at first. But the thing is, I would want to tell Don all this anyway, now that I know he's my cousin, so he might as well hear it now. And I don't mind if Liz knows. She already knows some of it."

"Well, tell it, then." Scarlatti sounded like she might be losing her patience.

Kim hurried into speech. "Okay. So anyway, my uncle had been saying for months that he was ready to buy. Aunt Mary had been working since my cousins started high school, and they'd saved up some money, and he'd been pressuring Naomi to set a price. I don't know why she didn't want to sell it. She was only there once in a while." Kim stopped and looked at us all. "And no matter what you say about Hannah, she gave Naomi her half of the business years ago, and I know she didn't take money for it. So she can be generous, you see."

Scarlatti and Daly exchanged looks.

Don straightened, and came over to Kim's side. "Just because no money was exchanged, doesn't mean that it wasn't a trade."

Kim looked confused. "I don't understand." Then her eyes widened. "You mean, it could have been like, blackmail? Hannah gave it to Naomi as a payment or something?"

"That's very astute." Hannah stood in the kitchen doorway with Richard Kendall behind her. "That's exactly how it was, Kim."

18

RICHARD Kendall made a sound of protest, and Hannah turned to him. "I know what you want me to do, and I'll do some of it. But it's time to clear the decks. Naomi was not a nice person, and there's no use sugarcoating the facts." She smiled a little, and moved into the room. "I'm not a nice person either, most of the time. But I don't really approve of lying."

Scarlatti spoke mildly. "Ms. Kershay has told us about the cake mix."

Hannah was magnificently unperturbed. "That was an emergency. I don't approve of cake mix either, but under the circumstances, I did what I had to do."

"Interesting." Scarlatti motioned Hannah to a chair in the circle before the fireplace. "Do you always respond to a crisis by compromising your ethics?"

Hannah's eyes narrowed. "I don't believe that remark was called for, Officer."

"I'm an inspector. That's what we call homicide investigators in San Francisco."

"How nice for you." Hannah sat on the sofa opposite the one where Bruno, Drake, and I were lined up like the three wise monkeys. She glared at Inspector Scarlatti.

"Did you want to hear what I have to say, or have you already made up your mind?"

Scarlatti gave her a measuring look. "I keep an open mind."

I felt like interjecting that her mind hadn't been so open when she'd labeled me as a likely suspect because of my ex-con status, but Drake's thigh had moved closer to mine, and I knew that was a signal to me to keep quiet. Besides, I was finding this mass interrogation fascinating. I didn't want them to decide to take down everyone's story separately.

Scarlatti and Daly walked away to talk together, probably debating that very point. Scarlatti came back and stood for a moment, examining us all. Kim, in the chair next to our sofa, and Don, sitting on the arm of her chair, looked back blankly. Hannah was at her haughtiest. Richard Kendall sat next to her, looking resigned.

"We have decided to continue talking to you in a group, because more of the pieces seem to come out this way. However, we may come to a point where we need to separate you. Until then, I'd like to pursue a couple of threads. Hannah, you said that Naomi blackmailed you into giving her your half of the take-out business you'd started together."

"Take-out and catering," Hannah corrected. "It had become quite a valuable business. Our overhead was lower than a restaurant, and the catering brought in a very nice income."

"So why did you turn it over?"

Hannah hesitated, and Mr. Kendall said, "You don't have to answer these questions. They haven't charged you. In fact, it's doubtful they have a case. Ms. Matthews may have died a natural death."

"No." Inspector Daly spoke up. "She was poisoned. The medical examiner is certain of it. They won't know what specifically caused her death until the toxicology testing is done—"

"And that will be a few weeks," Scarlatti put in.

"But because of certain signs, we are sure that her death was not a natural one. At this point, we are looking for the agent of death, the means by which the poison was administered. And of course, at who had opportunity, and who benefits."

"I have no objection to talking," Hannah said, disregarding her attorney's exasperated sigh. "I did nothing wrong. I have nothing to fear. And although there were times when I, well, when I hated Naomi, she was my business associate and closest friend for many years. I want to know who killed her." Her voice broke. "I miss her." She looked at us all defiantly. "It's true she did awful things, but I could understand why. And she was . . . important to me."

She took out a hankie—my hankie, I saw—and dabbed her eyes.

"So please tell us, if you don't mind," Scarlatti said, her voice polite, "about handing over your share of the profitable business you'd built together."

Hannah put away the hankie and took a deep breath. "She was really very naughty about that. You see, we'd been in college together, and I had once done something to make ends meet that would not really—" She paused, and looked helplessly at me.

"Enhance your legend."

Scarlatti frowned, but Hannah pounced on the phrase. "Exactly. It is not something I will discuss in a room full

184

of people, but I will be glad to tell you separately if you wish."

The inspectors exchanged glances. "We'll come back to it later," Scarlatti said. "At any rate, Naomi knew this thing you'd done. I presume it wasn't something illegal?"

"Not in the least," Hannah said, looking down her nose. "But I wasn't proud of doing it, and wouldn't have if there'd been any other way to earn enough to stay in college."

"So what happened?" Inspector Daly's quiet voice led her on. It occurred to me that he seemed content to take a backseat to Inspector Scarlatti's more flamboyant personality, but he managed to keep things moving in the right direction.

"I started to be very successful about ten years ago. That was when *Hannah Cooks for a Crowd* came out. I was approached for the TV show, and asked to write a syndicated column. Naomi resented my success. The fact is, she was never that creative. She could execute, but she had no vision. Kim knows that, don't you, Kim?"

Kim looked confused at being thus applied to. "I—I guess."

Hannah smiled at her approvingly. "It was plain to be seen. I gave Naomi a position of great responsibility in my new production company, but that didn't content her. Everything that came to me just made her angrier. Finally she said I should give her my half of the ownership in Beaned in Boston. That she had earned it, because I was too busy to take care of it anymore. Truly," Hannah said, sniffing, "she didn't do that much herself, because her brother Tony was very good at managing it and needed little guidance."

"So when she said that, what did you do?"

"I protested, of course." Hannah looked surprised. "After all, it was as much mine as hers in the first place— more, because my recipes were the basis of our business to begin with. However, I had begun to think that I would give it to her, that it was only fair, as I was growing away from it. I felt it didn't quite fit in with my other interests anymore."

"So where did the blackmail come in?" Inspector Scarlatti was impatient.

"Before I could say that I agreed with her, she sprung this scheme on me, that I would give her the company, or she would tell the world about my . . . indiscretion." Hannah realized that she had clenched her hands, and let them relax. "I told her I had already decided to let her have it, but that she would make me change my mind by her ridiculous demand. However, I knew she meant it."

She twisted one of her rings, not looking at us. "Well, I gave it to her. It wasn't worth the fight. But I'm afraid it set up a dangerous precedent. She assumed she had power over me. And in a way, she did. Because no one would care if I'd told the world that Naomi Matthews had had an illegitimate child with a married man."

Don made an inarticulate sound, and Hannah had the grace to look a little ashamed. "I'm sorry, Don. I will be glad to tell you everything I know about it later, if you want to know. Truthfully, I only met your father once. Naomi knew I didn't approve of her seeing a married man, so she kept him to herself."

"But what Naomi had done wouldn't be blackmail material?" Inspector Daly prodded gently.

"Who would care?" Hannah's shrug was eloquent. "But if she had dropped her little bombshell about me, it would have been the kind of news people love to dig up about celebrities. I would have weathered it, but it would have been unpleasant. So Naomi started to trade on that. When she wanted something from me, she would send me bits of her autobiography, in which everything she knew about me, and she knew a lot, was presented in the most unflattering terms."

"She did this recently?"

"She sent a section to the hotel, which I got when I arrived. And she left a few pages on the seat of the limo after the TV show. She wanted me to give her full credit for the crepe maker, to name it after her in the catalog, if you can imagine. How would that sell the product? The Naomi Matthews crepe maker." Hannah sounded scornful. "And besides, she had very little to do with its inception. Her one good idea was only part of the overall package."

"But she did think of part of it. I remember her saying so." Kim's forehead wrinkled.

"A very small part," Hannah said dismissively. "I had arranged a royalty for her, based on her participation in the product. It's the standard agreement with all my employees who contribute ideas to my line of products. They sign a contract. Naomi signed too. They agree that these products will be marketed under my name, that I have creative control. After all, they do much better that way than if they tried to take something to the marketplace without my name to sell it." Hannah was matter-of-fact about this, but I found myself wondering just how much of the stuff in her famous catalog was actually her own work.

"She wouldn't settle for this?" Scarlatti looked interested. "She thought you were cheating her?"

"She made it plain that she thought so. It put my back

up, and I decided to teach her she couldn't blackmail me like this." She looked around at all of us defiantly. "Last night, while she was sleeping off her drunk, I found her famous autobiography and I burned it."

19

THE inspectors exchanged glances. Beside me, Drake stirred restively, and I knew he wanted to ask his own questions. But he behaved, so I did too.

"And what was her response?"

"I don't think she'd noticed yet," Hannah said reflectively. "She was still unpleasantly triumphant this morning, like she really had me over the proverbial barrel."

"But you didn't feel threatened by that?" Scarlatti kept an eye on Richard Kendall when she made that statement, but Hannah went right on talking.

"Not in the least. I figured I would just destroy any other copies she might have, and make it clear to her I was preparing to pursue legal action if she published unflattering things about me. I decided I could discredit her if she actually went through with publishing something."

"Even though if she did publish a book, it would hold you up to ridicule in a very public way." Scarlatti managed to sound understanding and disbelieving at the same time.

"There are risks to any public life," Hannah said, shrugging. "You have to move on, or you're paralyzed."

"So what was the significance of the ivy and forget-me-nots?" Scarlatti asked the question casually, conversationally, as if it wasn't important.

Hannah's reaction made it clear that it was important. She looked at Richard Kendall for the first time.

"My client is under no obligation to answer," he began obediently.

"I thought you were going to be so frank and open," Scarlatti said, speaking directly to Hannah. "What is it about those flowers that makes you rethink that? Something that might incriminate you?"

"Bianca," Inspector Daly said. His voice was expressionless.

Scarlatti looked at him, her lips pressed together. Then she turned back to Hannah. "We're ready to take you into the other room, if you don't feel comfortable in this situation."

Hannah took a deep breath. "Why bother," she said bitterly. "No doubt this will all come out anyway. The flowers, Inspector," and she gave the title a sarcastic emphasis, "have a very personal meaning for me. My husband, Morton, used to send me such an arrangement on our anniversary every year. He was quite sentimental. He said the ivy was our love, entwining each of us, and the forget-me-nots were a pledge that we would always be together." She pressed her lips tightly, and brought out the hankie again. "He was a very good, very dear man."

"So is he still sending you flowers?" Scarlatti didn't seem impressed by the hankie and the speech Hannah gave.

"He died almost two years ago." Hannah managed to infuse quiet outrage into her voice.

"So the flowers weren't from him. Who sent them, and why?"

"Naomi, of course." Hannah spoke sharply. "That

was her new threat. She would make people think I had killed my husband if I didn't fall into line. If she had ever married, maybe that's the kind of thing she would do, bump off her husband at the drop of a hat. But I had a wonderful relationship with my husband, Inspector. He was the love of my life."

"How did he die?" Scarlatti sounded interested.

"He was on a business trip in the Far East. I had given him strict instructions about what he could eat, but he was . . . easily tempted."

"Slipped the leash, did he?"

"Really, Inspector!"

"Bianca—"

"I must insist," Richard Kendall said, "that you treat my client's feelings with more respect."

"Sorry." Scarlatti didn't look sorry. "Please continue."

"He was ill when he got home, and he wouldn't go to the hospital until it was too late." Hannah looked troubled. "In a way, I blame myself. I was busy with the launch of our Web site, and didn't insist that he take care of himself soon enough. If I had only been home more—if I had only just put him right into the car and taken him over to his internist, perhaps he would still be alive." She plied the hankie again. "He would certainly be horrified to know that Naomi used his death as another stick to beat me with."

"So why did she think you had killed him, if he died from food poisoning?" Inspector Daly asked the question in his quiet way.

"She didn't think so, really. She just wanted me to see how the most innocent things could be turned into nasty gossip." Hannah's mouth twisted. "All that about poison mushrooms. It was ridiculous, and she knew it. Morton didn't even like mushrooms. He wouldn't have eaten them under any circumstances. He died in the hospital, with doctors in attendance. They raised no questions whatsoever about his death. Unless Naomi knew something I didn't know, there was nothing in his death but a personal tragedy for me."

We were silent for a moment. "Bianca?" Inspector Daly stood, and walked across the room with his colleague.

Bruno and Drake looked at each other across me. I was longing to know what they thought of the unorthodox methods Inspector Scarlatti was employing, but guessed they wouldn't say anything until we headed back to Palo Alto.

At least it didn't appear that I was at the top of the suspect list anymore. It seemed to me that they were drawing a net around Hannah, one she might find it difficult to wriggle out of, even with Richard Kendall's help.

He thought so too. He spoke to his client in a low voice, but we could hear.

"You shouldn't be volunteering all this information," he exhorted her. "Let them do their own discovery. No use handing them motive after motive on a silver platter."

"Nonsense," Hannah said firmly. She didn't bother to lower her voice more than a notch. "I've given them nothing that everyone else here didn't know something about." She caught my eye. "Although it appears Liz was surprisingly restrained in her talk with them. Thank you, Liz."

Drake gave me a cold stare. "We don't think your restraint was so admirable."

"Hannah told us those things in confidence. I couldn't reveal them. In fact, I bet Bridget didn't blab in her statement either, did she?"

He ignored that. He had always had a soft spot for

Bridget, and wasn't nearly so rigorous in his demands on her. "And if they'd arrested you?"

"That would have been a different story. I'd have thrown her to the wolves without a second thought."

Hannah actually laughed. "As I've decided to make a clean breast of it all, your discretion no longer matters. But I thank you. I am not used to finding so much"—she hesitated over the word—"loyalty in someone who is not even my own employee. If you lived on the East Coast, I would offer you a job."

"That's generous." I thought I would exercise some of my little-used tact and not mention that nothing short of absolute penury would induce me to work for her.

The inspectors came back. "We're going to continue for the moment," Scarlatti said. "I'm sorry this is taking so long. Perhaps we can wrap it up soon." She smiled at Drake and Bruno. "I'm sure you're getting hungry."

As soon as she said the word "hungry," my stomach growled. It was nearly seven; lunch had been skimpy, and dinner looked like it wouldn't happen at all.

"Perhaps we could have some food sent up," Hannah suggested.

"I couldn't eat," Kim said. "It's too upsetting." She nearly sobbed on the last word. Don stroked her hair absently, as if he didn't realize what an intimate gesture that was.

Scarlatti shook her head at Hannah's suggestion. "If you don't mind waiting a little longer," she said, smiling nicely, "I'd like to just get on with it."

I didn't know what to make of her sudden politeness. Perhaps Inspector Daly had told her that she'd catch more flies with honey than with vinegar. He, I noticed, was no longer in the room. I could hear crunching, and realized he was in the kitchen. He must have been phoning; we could just barely hear his voice.

"To continue," Scarlatti said, turning her attention to Kim. "You were going to tell us about your uncle's death."

"Can't you just get that from the Boston police?" Hannah evidently wasn't charmed by Scarlatti's new leaf.

"We have requested the paperwork," Scarlatti said. "But since you were the one who made this accusation, perhaps you could start by telling us why?"

"Why?"

"Why you accused Naomi of having caused her brother's death."

"Well," Hannah said, stalling. "It wasn't a particularly nice thing to say. I didn't really think so, you understand. I just wanted Naomi to see what it felt like to have someone make stuff up about you."

"And how did she react? You were in your dressing room at the TV station, is that right?" Scarlatti consulted her notebook.

"Yes. After the show. She was helping me take off that awful makeup." Hannah frowned. "Actually, I was surprised. I had expected her to dismiss it, to tell me it was just as true that she'd poisoned her brother as that I had killed poor Morton. But she didn't say that. She flew into an even greater rage, if you want the truth."

Scarlatti made a note. Then she turned back to Kim. "The day before your uncle's death, he and your aunt had a terrible fight, you said. Tell me about that."

Kim took a deep breath. "I was out front, setting up the salad case. We weren't open yet. Aunt Naomi had come in about ten minutes earlier, and she and my uncle had gone back to the office in the back of the shop. He was smiling, and I thought she was finally there to talk about him assuming ownership. Then we heard all this yelling. My grandmother was Italian," Kim added, glancing uncertainly at Scarlatti. "Yelling wasn't that unusual."

"I'm Italian, and I know what you mean." Scarlatti smiled.

"But—you're blond." Kim stopped. "I'm sorry—"

"There are blond Italians too," Scarlatti said lightly. "So go on with your story. Some heavy-duty Italian yelling was going on. Could you tell what about?"

"Yes," Kim said ingenuously, "because we all went back and stood in the hall."

"All? How many people?"

"Me and Roxanne and Karen. Karen is my uncle Tony's oldest," Kim said, with a glance at Don. "She goes to BU and only helps in the shop part-time."

"So what were they saying?"

"Naomi yelled about him not having the balls for owning anything, and he yelled that she was a mean, bitter bitch, and she yelled that it was a good thing she was a bitch, because he let everyone walk all over him, and you couldn't run a business like that, and he yelled that if she was really in charge, no one would work there because she was so awful, and she said he would never have lasted an instant at a real job, and he said if she didn't work for a woman as nasty as she was, she wouldn't have lasted an instant either." Kim glanced apologetically at Hannah. "Sorry. That's what he said. Then she slapped him."

Kim and Hannah both looked at me. "She had a good slapping arm on her," I said.

"She could lose control," Kim said. "She got so angry

195

sometimes. Anyway, my uncle said he'd never hit a woman yet, but if she didn't get out of his office, he'd make an exception for her. And she said it wouldn't be his office long." Kim shivered. "There was a silence, and then Uncle Tony said, in a kind of weary way, that if he quit, her business would never recover, because no one else would work as hard as he had for as little as she paid. I think that part was true." Kim fell silent.

"So how did it end?" Scarlatti asked the question we all wanted to know.

"Naomi said he'd have a hard time quitting if she fired him, and Uncle Tony said she was welcome to try and fire him, but they had an agreement, and he'd see her in court. And that was the end of it. She stormed out."

"So tell me, if you can, about the day your uncle died. The next day, was it?" Scarlatti sounded almost gentle as she asked that question.

"The very next morning." Kim sniffed. "Roxanne found him, which is lucky, because otherwise it would have been Karen, and that would have been so awful. Roxanne was there early to prep the salads, and she went back to tell Uncle Tony to make sure he got some more mayo. He wasn't at his desk, like he usually was."

"He came in early too?"

Kim nodded. "Oh, he was always the first one there, every morning. Sometimes before eight. We didn't open until ten, though he was thinking of putting in an espresso machine and opening for the commuter rush, because so many people would knock early, when it was just him, asking if we had coffee. He went in at that time to get some of the paperwork and stuff out of the way."

"So when Roxanne didn't see him there," Scarlatti prodded, "what did she do?"

"She saw him." Kim gulped. "He wasn't at the desk, but she noticed something on the floor behind the desk, kind of sticking out, she said. And when she went around, there he was, just lying there, all slumped over, like he'd fallen out of his chair."

"On his face, or on his back?" The question came from Drake. Immediately he reddened, and said to the inspector, "Sorry, Bianca."

"It's a good question," she said, smiling at him. "Do you know, Kim?"

"I don't . . . well, wait a minute. Roxanne said something about not realizing he was dead until she'd pushed his shoulder. So he must have been on his face." She looked from Drake to Scarlatti. "Why does that matter?"

Scarlatti gestured at Drake. "Tell her, maestro."

"If he'd had a heart attack, fallen over like that on his front, a certain amount of lividity would be present in his face because of his body's position. If he'd been on his back and there'd been lividity, it might have alerted the coroner to look at the death more closely."

"It's a bit technical," Scarlatti said, seeing the confusion on Kim's face. "But it means they'd be more likely to overlook some signs of poisoning, like a flushed face and spittle on the lips, because gravity would have naturally caused those things if he'd died normally."

"His doctor was surprised, but not much." Kim wiped her eyes with the back of her hand. "He said he'd told Uncle Tony a million times if he'd told him once, cut out the fat and get some exercise."

"Had your aunt been there since the quarrel the previous day?" Scarlatti put the question.

"I don't know. I hadn't seen her. But everyone knew Uncle Tony came in a couple of hours before the rest of us. Roxanne got there at ten that morning, and usually none of us were there until ten-thirty." Kim gazed at the inspector, at Drake and Bruno. "Is it true? Did she kill her own brother?"

"We don't know." Scarlatti looked at her with pity. "Probably the Boston ME's office will exhume your uncle's body—"

"Well, he was cremated," Kim exclaimed. "That's what he and my aunt both have in their wills. He was cremated, and we had a memorial service." Her face darkened. "Aunt Naomi even spoke, and said what a wonderful brother he was, and cried crocodile tears that they had parted on bad terms. When I think of that, I don't care that she's dead. I don't care at all!"

We were all silent for a moment. Outside the balcony windows, the soft glow of an overcast San Francisco night filled the sky; the lights of many buildings reflected off the fog to make a kind of perpetual twilight.

"Well, I care." Don spoke, drawing himself a little away from Kim. "I never had a chance to know what kind of woman she was. Maybe she was a hard-nosed business person. That's not so uncommon." He looked at Hannah. "But she might have been something different underneath, something she never had a chance to express. You don't know she did that awful thing." He caught our eyes on him and flushed, the color standing out patchily on his lean cheeks. "Kim told you my mother—my adoptive mother—died last year. Liver cancer. She was great. I felt guilty after she died that I'd wondered, since I was little, about my birth mother, about how special she must be. I was thinking about doing one of those Internet searches for her, if you want the truth." He looked back down at his hands. "Now, I guess I just feel doubly cheated."

Kim began to cry, softly. Don patted her shoulder awkwardly. "Hey, I didn't mean to make you feel bad. And like you say, I've got cousins and uncles and aunts I never knew I had. My family—my adoptive family—was just me and my mom and Granny Ellen, after my dad walked out. I'm glad to find I've got some connections."

Inspector Daly appeared at the kitchen door. He gestured to Scarlatti, and she went over for another of their low-voiced conferences. Don got up and went into the foyer to use the powder room. Kim remained huddled in her chair.

I felt stiff from sitting, so I stretched a little. "Will it be much longer?"

Drake and Bruno exchanged glances. "I could not say." Bruno shrugged. "She is very unorthodox, our Bianca. She must have some end in mind, to pool the interviews like this."

"She's got something up her sleeve," Drake agreed, watching Bianca push a lock of blond hair behind her ear. "Never so fetching as when she's planning a coup."

Richard Kendall had seized his opportunity to talk to Hannah. He tapped a forefinger forcibly on his palm, making points. She listened, nodding, but there was a mulish cast to her mouth. After a moment she told him, "Excuse me," and went over to the phone on the library desk, where she spoke for some time.

Scarlatti and Inspector Daly came over to join us. "What's Hannah doing?" Scarlatti scowled at Richard

Kendall. "She can't be calling her attorney, because you're here."

He gazed calmly back at her. "You haven't charged her with anything. You have no right to stop her from making a phone call."

"I have every right, if she's calling the media." Scarlatti strode over to the library desk as Hannah put down the phone.

"I have ordered us a meal," Hannah said, her chin raised. "We are all tired and hungry, and will think better if we get something to eat. I asked them to send it right up. It should be here in minutes. If you will tell your officers, Inspector? I suppose they will want to examine the food for files, or something of that nature."

"This is highly unorthodox," Scarlatti said.

"You can say that? My attorney assures me you are conducting this investigation in a highly unorthodox way. Breaking bread with your suspects will just be more of the same." Hannah smiled blandly. "Or if you prefer, you can watch us eat." She inclined her head graciously to Bruno. "Please do join us, Detective Morales." Her smile was less gracious when she turned it to Drake. "Detective Drake."

Neither of them said they would eat, though Bruno murmured a thank-you for the invitation.

I was peckish. When the knock on the door came, and the room-service waiter wheeled in his cart, the room filled with savory aromas and I was sure we would all have to eat.

"It's just a simple meal," Hannah said, tipping the waiter and shutting the door behind him. "Sandwiches, soup, and some cookies. Do join us." She set the food out on one end of the large table. "We'll dine buffet style, so you can continue to grill us."

I went into the powder room when Don came out, and took a moment to comb my hair, which is not long and blond, but short and an indeterminate brown, and incapable of being tossed in that coquettish way so many women seem born knowing. Looking in the mirror, I could hardly believe that Drake would choose me over someone like Bianca Scarlatti. But he had. He did. It gave me an incredible sense of well-being, to counterbalance all the angst I had felt earlier.

When I got back into the drawing room, people had gathered around the food. It was a nice spread, and Hannah had set it out with an eye to appearances. Plates and soup cups at one side, a silver tureen, a platter of sandwich triangles, a plate of raw vegetables and fruit. The soup smelled wonderful.

Drake and Bruno had helped themselves and were standing with Scarlatti and Daly over beside the library desk; Daly ate his sandwich in quick, hungry bites. Don, plate in hand, had been drawn down to sit next to Hannah. She talked earnestly, and I guessed she was giving him a picture of Naomi that might ameliorate the one he'd received in the past few hours.

I was ready to make my selections, but as I stood ladling soup into a cup, my eye caught a faint movement out on the balcony, and at the same moment, I realized Kim wasn't in the room.

I thought perhaps she needed some time alone. I was reluctant to draw official attention to that need, but it made me uneasy. I put down the ladle and went to the tall windows that opened onto the balcony.

Something was wrong. Kim was out there, but she wasn't standing, leaning on the railing, as she had the previous day. She was up on the wide parapet, clinging to the railing that ran down the middle of it. She looked perilously close to the edge.

20

I wanted to shriek for Drake, for anyone to come and take charge of this dangerous situation. But I knew from listening to Drake and Bruno talk about their cases that often a person who looks like they're about to jump only jumps when people yell at them not to. I didn't want to precipitate Kim's suicidal action.

Instead I slipped out quietly through one leaf of the window, leaving it open to alert those in the room behind to what was happening. How had they let it happen? How had they lost track of Kim?

However it happened, it had to be dealt with. I only hoped I could help matters instead of making them worse.

My eyes grew used to the dim light. In the city glare, reflected off the foggy overcast of a San Francisco January, I could see Kim crouched on the parapet. She was still on my side of the railing, hugging the iron bars, staring down at the city street thirty stories below.

I was almost beside her before she sensed the movement behind her and turned to see me.

"Hey, Kim. There's food inside." I tried to sound matter-of-fact, noncommittal, unthreatening. My voice wanted badly to shake. "Why don't you come and have some soup?"

Her face in the light from the window was pinched. "I can't," she whispered. "Don't come any closer, Liz."

I was only a foot away by that time. "Okay," I said, at my most soothing. "Say, that doesn't look too safe. Come down and tell me why you can't have soup with us."

"I just can't. I'm not coming down." Still she crouched, her arms wrapped around a couple of the metal rails. The railing was about three feet tall. If she stood, she could topple over it easily, or just step over.

There was movement at the window behind me, blocking the light from the room. Drake's voice said, "Liz? What—"

"Kim and I are talking out here." I didn't turn to face him. I didn't take my eyes off Kim. "She doesn't want to come in and eat with us."

"Leave me alone," Kim said, the childish words taking on a new resonance. "Just let me alone! I can't—I just can't . . ."

"What can't you do?" I wanted to reach to her, touch her shoulder. It was an effort to keep my hands to myself. "Tell me. Let me help you. I'm your friend, Kim. I thought I was."

"You won't be," she said breathily. "No one will be. I thought I could handle it. I thought—but I can't. I can't live with this!"

"I don't understand."

She clung, trembling, to the rail, and I began to be afraid that nothing I could do would get her down. All the light from the room was gone now; I imagined the others standing clustered in front of the french window, sandwiches forgotten. I could hear Scarlatti talking on her cell phone. Perhaps she knew a surefire way to get suicidal people back from the brink. The city police probably had a lot of experience with that. After all, the Golden Gate Bridge had a lot of jumpers every year.

Kim was silent. I said, moving forward a tiny inch, "Kim, please come down. This is no resolution to anything. It hurts too many people who love you. Come down and we'll figure out a way to solve the problem, whatever it is."

"Don't you know? Haven't you guessed?" Her voice rose hysterically. "I thought for sure you would guess, Liz."

Scarlatti spoke from behind me. "Kim, you come down this instant." She sounded calm, but just the tiniest bit angry.

Kim scrambled to her feet, towering over me. The railing was hip-high on her; no problem for her to swing her leg over and take the final plunge. "Don't you come closer! Don't anyone come closer!" Her voice rose in alarm. From the room behind me came a series of agitated murmurs.

"No one will come closer, Kim." I wanted so badly to just reach out and pluck her down, but she would struggle, and that might be all it took to push her over the edge. She was young and strong, taller than I was.

She seemed to teeter as she stood, outlined against the night sky. "I don't want to die," she sobbed. "But I have to. I have to."

"Why?" Scarlatti's voice came from over my shoulder. "You didn't kill anyone, did you?"

Kim was staring down at the street as if mesmerized. She swayed, leaning over the railing.

"Kim," I babbled, trying to wrest her attention from

that dangerous plunge. "Kim, please tell me about it. I will still be your friend. I've done a bad thing or two in my life, and yet people are still willing to be my friend. I've been wanting to pass that on. I'll pass it on to you."

She had turned to look at me, and beyond me, into the room. I didn't dare turn to see who was behind me, besides Scarlatti. I had the irrational fear that if I took my eyes off her for a moment, she would lose her grip and go over.

"Okay," she said after a moment. "But you have to leave." She spoke to the spectators. "Only Liz. I'll only talk to Liz."

"Kim," Scarlatti began. "I'll just listen. I won't say anything. But I want to be here too."

"No!" Kim's voice regained that edge of hysteria. "You leave!"

"Okay, okay." Scarlatti sounded farther away. "All you people, back off. She wants room."

"She's not armed, is she?" That was Drake. He sounded calm, but I could hear the worry in his voice.

"I'm assuming not."

Light from the room poured onto the balcony again. I pictured Hannah and her lawyer, Drake and Bruno, Don and the San Francisco detectives, all standing back from the window, watching as if it were a poorly lit play. I hoped they'd figured out a way to help me that didn't involve just holding a net open on the street to try and catch Kim.

"They're gone, aren't they?" I inched a little closer to her. "We can talk now."

She caught her breath and turned away to look down into the street again.

"Kim, why don't you sit down again? That will be

more comfortable. I'm worried about you, and you make me feel very short when you are so far above me."

She thought about that for a minute, then she nodded. "Okay. I don't want you to feel short, Liz. I mean, you are short, so it would be rude to make you feel shorter."

"I appreciate that."

Still clutching the railing, she let herself down until she once more crouched on the parapet. "Is that better?"

"Well, best of all would be for you to sit at this table with me." I gestured to the small iron table and bistro chairs that graced the balcony. "Or come inside. It's cold out here."

"I can't." She shook her head wildly, and her hair flew out. "You don't know, Liz. I have to be punished. Maybe even die."

"Tell me what's so bad, Kim. Nothing can be that bad."

"You don't know," she said again. "Can they hear me in there?"

"I don't think so."

"Good." She hugged herself. It was probably forty-five degrees out there, but at least there was no wind.

"Okay, Liz, I'll tell you what I did. And you'll agree. I know you will. I did something very bad."

"I'm listening." I moved a little closer. She didn't notice.

"I gave . . ." Her voice was hesitant. "I gave Naomi the wrong glass."

"This morning?"

Kim nodded. "It's all mixed up, and at first I didn't realize what I'd done. I was so busy with making sure we had everything we needed for the day, it just didn't sink in."

I thought of all those white boxes of cinnamon roll-ups, destined to be uneaten by Hannah's fans.

"So you think there was something in the glass, something Naomi put in it?"

"When she knocked over her drink, that made me wonder. I mean, I could tell she knocked it over on purpose, and I thought it was just to be devilish."

She stopped, and I nodded encouragement. "She could be very devilish."

"You know she went and got a fresh glass of water while we were cleaning up. When she set down the new drink on the coffee table, I realized she'd switched them so Hannah would get her glass."

She stopped. I waited a moment. "Did you think she was trying to play a trick on Hannah?"

She leaned closer to me. "That's exactly what I thought! That's what anyone would think, right? I figured she had put something in the glass to give Hannah the runs or make her feel awful. I never dreamed she wanted to kill Hannah. I didn't believe that about my uncle, you see. We all knew he had a heart attack. No one ever had the least suspicion, and when Hannah said it, I just put it down to them being angry, like Naomi saying Hannah killed her husband with bad mushrooms."

"So you assumed Naomi wanted Hannah to get humiliatingly sick or something."

"Right." Kim's voice was shaking. "So I just—pushed her glass closer to her."

"And Naomi didn't notice? You'd think she'd keep a sharp eye on the poison."

Kim shook her head. "She was ranting at Hannah. I was even . . ." She shuddered. I could sense the movement from where I stood. I longed to put my arm around her. "I was even giggling inside to think that it would be Naomi with the runs, not Hannah. After all, we needed Hannah to be able to do her job, but Naomi was just being trouble."

She caught her breath. "Oh, God, how can I talk about her like that? My own aunt. And I killed her!"

"You didn't kill her." I did move that time, and put a hand on Kim's arm. She didn't flinch. "She killed herself with her own wickedness. If she hadn't put poison in that glass, nothing would have happened."

"But why didn't I just take it and pour it out? Why didn't I stop it?"

Kim put back her head and wailed. "It's on my hands. Her death is on my hands!"

I grabbed her arm, but she surged upward, nearly dislocating my shoulder. "Kim, you can't take this on yourself. Truly, it belongs on Naomi's plate and no other. The harm she would have done to another, she did to herself."

Kim didn't hear me. She stood, her legs braced against the railing, her head lifted to the sky. "It was my fault. None of this would have happened if not for me!"

I grabbed her legs and held on. "Kim, please. Don't do this. Your family will be so upset."

"My family." Kim let a hysterical giggle go. "My mom would be horrified to know what I did. It will all come out. She'll be so humiliated by my behavior. I can't face them. I can't tell them what I've done."

Her leg muscles tensed. I knew she would jump. I held on for all I was worth.

"I'm not going to let you go, Kim. You'll have to take me with you. Is that what you want?"

"Let go. I don't want to hurt you too, Liz." She

twisted, and I felt her overbalance. She screamed. My heart nearly stopped.

I pulled back as hard as I could, trying to counteract the force of her impetus. At that moment, I felt that she wanted to claw her way back, but her center of gravity was too far out. I tightened my grip on her legs, fighting her own panic and uncertainty. Every move she made counteracted what I was trying to do. I shouted for help, wondering why none of the people in the room behind us was coming to my aid.

"Kim." It was Don's voice. He might have been lanky, but he was strong. He reached over my head, grabbed her around the waist, and lifted her down.

She clung to him, sobbing.

"I can't afford to lose any more of my new relatives," he said to her, cradling her in his arms.

"But it was my fault. I killed her, Don. I killed your mother. You never got to know her because of me." Kim cried uncontrollably, her breath coming in hiccuping sobs.

Don smoothed the hair off her face. "I heard what you said. My birth mother was a deeply unhappy woman. It's enough that she committed suicide. You shouldn't make it worse by doing that too."

He carried her inside, and I followed. My teeth were chattering like castanets; I shivered uncontrollably. It would be good to get out of the cold, foggy night, and into the warmth.

21

MY arms began to ache before I'd finished the restorative cup of tea Drake insisted I drink. I had exerted myself beyond my normal strength to try and pull Kim away from the railing, and I would feel it for a few days.

Kim was having a cup of tea too. I only knew that because Hannah herself had carried it to Kim's bedroom, where Scarlatti and Daly were taking her statement. We had finished with the group stuff; I suppose it had served its purpose, though it was hard to say what. If they had concentrated on Kim, taken her off by herself, would she not have broken down and admitted her part in the death of her aunt without feeling obliged to toss herself from the top floor of the hotel? I thought she would. But this way had gotten results too, at the expense of some very anxious moments.

"When will you stop putting yourself out there like that, woman?" Drake poured more sugar in my tea.

"It's undrinkable already," I protested.

"You need the sugar for shock." His fierce expression might not be interpreted by others as loving concern, but I chose to interpret it that way.

Bruno nodded. "Paolo is right. You worry your friends when you take such risks. Drink your tea."

We were back in our places on the couch. Hannah was in the kitchen, redeeming her reputation as domestic goddess by heating up the soup. Its savory aroma made me remember that I'd had nothing to eat since the cheese and crackers Bridget had served. Well, a few of her cookies as well. But that had been hours ago. It was nearly nine, and we still weren't finished.

"What's next?" Don sat across from us, his face creased with worry. "Will they arrest Kim?"

"They could," Drake said reluctantly, "because she withheld information in a murder investigation. But I doubt they will."

"And Richard Kendall is in there," I added. "He'll keep them at bay."

We had all been surprised when Hannah had offered the services of her attorney to Kim. But it was only fair. Hannah must have been feeling the breeze from the wings of the angel of death. If not for Kim, Hannah would be dead instead of Naomi.

That knowledge seemed to have shaken her. But she dealt with it by bustling around the kitchen, a response I understood, because Bridget reacted the same way to stress.

Don still looked worried. "It's not like she meant to hurt anyone," he argued, though there was no use arguing with us—we were already converted.

"They'll take that into account. If they decide to declare it accidental death, or death by misadventure, there'll be no repercussions for Kim. Otherwise, she might have to be arraigned on a charge of involuntary manslaughter, but a good lawyer could probably get that dismissed or commuted."

Don plowed his fingers through his hair. "Poor Kim.

She's so overcome by it. Doesn't seem fair that such a harmless thing should have such long-range consequences."

"She'll be okay. She'll get over it," Drake said. "She's young. Once she gets back home with her folks, it'll fade. After all, Naomi more than likely did cause her brother's death, and the whole family will probably have a harder time forgiving that than forgiving what Kim did."

"What about you?" I probably shouldn't have said anything, but I was curious about Don's reaction to his newfound family. "Will you go back to Massachusetts and meet them?"

"I don't know." He looked uneasy. "Given what Naomi did, it's no great recommendation to be her son, is it?"

"If Kim is any example of that family, I think you can count on a warm welcome." I smiled at him over the cup of too-sweet tea. "She's really something special."

"Yeah. Maybe Naomi was the anomaly, not the norm." He brightened a little. Then his smile faded. "Do you think they'll investigate Kim's uncle's death now? I don't really want my birth mother branded a murderer, even if she deserved it."

"Probably not." Drake looked at Bruno.

"I would not think so, though of course it is not my jurisdiction," Bruno said thoughtfully. "It is all hearsay, isn't it? Naomi is dead, and the body of her supposed victim has been cremated. There is no proof. Why go to the trouble and expense of investigating that?"

"I'm wondering what poison she used." I set the tea down, hoping to distract Drake from my failure to drink it.

Bruno shrugged. "Without tissue samples and stomach contents, it is difficult to say. But tell me, do you know if she had cats or dogs, or any kind of pet?"

"Sheesh, I don't know."

Don spoke up. "She did have cats. She called from the airport to talk to them on her answering machine."

"Oh, right. She did that here too." I looked at Bruno curiously. "Why? Should we let someone know to take care of them?"

"I would bet that Kim will soon be caring for her aunt's cats," Bruno said. "But I ask because it is possible to use certain flea repellents as a poison, if you know how to do it."

"And she did have a degree in chemistry, let's remember."

Don leaned forward. "So you think she used flea repellent?"

"Only certain kinds work." Bruno smiled. "And I will not tell you what kinds, in case you become homicidal, Don. But given the way in which her death occurred, it seems likely to me."

"Bruno's the toxicologist," Drake said. "He just took a couple of courses, didn't you, my man?"

"I have studied a little." Bruno waved away Drake's words. "It is not possible to be a toxicologist without much more study than I have done, Paolo."

"Incredible." Don shook his head. "That she would plan to do such things. It makes me even more grateful for the way I was raised by my adoptive mom. We were poor, but she gave me everything I needed."

"You were lucky then." I pushed the cup of tea farther away on the table when I leaned forward to pat Don's hand.

"I didn't always know it." He looked down at his hands. "I made trouble when I was a teenager. Was sure that because I was adopted, no one loved me. Didn't help that my dad—my adoptive dad—bailed on us a couple of

214

years before that." His hands clenched, and he looked up, staring at us with deep gray eyes—Naomi's eyes, I suddenly realized. "By God, no kid of mine will ever have to wonder if his dad loves him."

"Then your children will be lucky." Drake stood and clapped Don on the shoulder. "That soup is making me hungry. What say we go see if we can get some?"

"Good idea." I started to get up too.

"Not you, mate." Drake pushed me back onto the couch. "You're staying right here. You're not moving an inch, no matter if you see Godzilla rampaging through the streets of San Francisco. Did you get a sandwich earlier?"

"I got no food at all." I made my voice as plaintive as possible. "And I'm very hungry."

"I'll be glad to serve you, milady." He treated me to a grin. "And while you wait, you can finish that tea."

I enjoyed the feeling of being cherished. I didn't actually want to be treated that way most of the time; I like my independence, standing on my own two feet, beholden to no one. But danger and stress affect each of us differently. It had made Don unnaturally loquacious. It threatened to turn me into a marshmallow of a woman who had to be pampered and waited on. I wondered how soon it would pass, and who would tire of it first—Drake, or me.

Bruno said, "The tea, Liz."

I jumped. "Thought you went with the soup brigade."

"They will not need me." He leaned closer. "So you and Paolo have fixed things?"

I didn't pretend not to understand him. "I'm not sure. I think we still have some hammering out to do. His reaction this afternoon was totally over the top. I can't deal with that."

"He cares very much, and his way of expressing it is to yell."

"I don't like yelling."

Bruno shrugged. "In any lasting relationship, there will be times of anger. It's not whether you get angry at each other that matters. It's how you work through it, and whether you let it drive a wedge between you."

"So are you taking classes in marriage counseling as well?"

He looked abashed. "Not exactly. I speak from experience, you understand. Lucy is a counselor, and she has told me some of it. But also, we have been married for over fifteen years. In that time, we have learned something about how to handle the other person."

I wasn't really comfortable talking about this with a man who wasn't Drake. But at the same time, Bruno knew his work partner probably better than anyone else, including me. "Bruno, there are things I just can't accept from any man, and one of them is this overbearing male behavior. It sets up very unpleasant echoes for me."

"And yet you accept Paolo's concern, and that he expresses it by ordering you to wait to be served, by trying to make you take things easy. It is his nature to show his care this way."

"I know. But it's my nature to find that difficult to be around."

Bruno looked troubled. "You will find a way to compromise. You must, because each of you is completed by the other one."

I stared at him, mouth agape. "What ever makes you say that?"

"It is true." He shrugged. "I have known it since soon after he met you. He has known it for nearly that long.

You, I think, struggle against the knowledge. Perhaps you could have gone through life without him, never missing what he could bring to you. But now, I think, you begin to understand that you are bound to him, as he is to you."

"You must be taking shrink lessons," I muttered. "Either that, or you've been listening to your wife too much."

"I speak only what I see," Bruno said, drawing himself up. "In this case, evidently you have blinded yourself, Liz, because you too are capable of seeing this. If you choose not to acknowledge your feelings, that is your problem. But in this case, it becomes my friend Paolo's problem, and that makes me apprehensive for him."

"Soup's on." Drake came through the kitchen door, carrying the tureen carefully between oven-mitted hands. "It's nice and hot. I'll bring you a cup, Liz. Bruno?"

"I will serve myself," Bruno said. He smiled at me. "But I know Liz appreciates your care of her."

I cleared my throat. "Of course I do. Thanks, Paul."

22

WE sat around in the beautiful room, drinking our soup. Don had soup too, slurping it up moodily. I ate three of the sandwich triangles, despite their somewhat dry bread. Nothing ever tasted better. Hannah joined us, but she kept throwing glances over her shoulder at the kitchen and the bedrooms beyond it.

"When will they be done?" She tore a piece of the stale bread into crumbs. "Poor Kim is having quite an ordeal."

"What will happen to the shop, anyway?" I looked at her over my second cup of soup. "Beaned in Boston. Who'll run it now?"

"I don't know." Hannah seemed struck. "Let's see, Naomi and I each made a will a couple of years ago, and many of our business concerns were left to each other, to obviate any legal problems arising out of either of our deaths. I might inherit the shop from her. Or it might go to her next of kin, which would be—"

We all looked at Don. He looked alarmed.

"It wouldn't be me. I don't think I could inherit unless she acknowledged me as her son, and she hadn't done that."

"She might have, but I agree, she was unlikely to unless she'd told you about it." Hannah patted Don's hand.

"Your mother was a bit manipulative, you know. She would have wanted you to be properly grateful for anything she chose to give you."

"I didn't need anything from her. I still don't. But wouldn't her next of kin be her brothers and sisters? Like, my aunts and uncles? Kim said there were several."

"I think you might be right," Drake said. "Maybe Richard Kendall would know."

"The laws in Massachusetts are different from California," Hannah announced, her tone of voice making it clear that Massachusetts's laws were far superior. "I will call my attorney and ask him."

"No need, not right now." Don held up a hand. "I just wondered, because it occurred to me that Kim would be good at running that thing. From what she was telling me on the plane, she knows everything but the paperwork, and a good accountant could help her with that until she catches on. I think she'd like to keep it in the family."

"That's very thoughtful of you, Don." Hannah gave him her most gracious, most motherly smile. "I'm certain I can arrange that. After all, Kim saved my life."

"I wouldn't mention that part, if I were you." I pushed my soup cup away. "Kim doesn't regard that as her most shining hour."

"I shall be tactful, of course," Hannah said.

We all exchanged glances, wondering if she knew how.

Kim's bedroom door opened, and Scarlatti came crunching through the kitchen, followed by Daly, Kim, and Mr. Kendall.

Hannah made a sound of annoyance. "Inspector, when can we have that mess cleaned up? I can't tell you how distressing it is to try to work in a kitchen full of broken glass and other assorted rubbish."

219

"I can imagine." Scarlatti looked around at us, a measuring look. "We're about to wrap up our investigation. You'll be glad to know that we've decided to bring it in as accidental death. Your statements will all be used, and you may be asked to return to testify, but the likelihood is that this ends your involvement. As our evidence procurement is at an end, you may have your kitchen cleaned without further ado."

Drake spoke. "And what about Liz? She was abducted at gunpoint. Will you file charges in that case?"

Everyone looked at me. I looked at Hannah.

"I'm sorry I did that, Liz." Hannah looked abashed, but I wondered cynically how good she was at calling up whatever emotion seemed currently useful. "All I can say is my mind was most unsettled by Naomi's death. If there's any way I can make it up to you . . ."

"Ms. Sullivan may, of course, press charges." Scarlatti didn't sound too enthusiastic about it. Prosecuting Hannah Couch probably struck her as a public relations nightmare.

"I'm not going to press charges." I had meant to string Hannah along for a while, make her sweat in return for the damage she'd done my livelihood, but the words popped out of my mouth. Sometimes my mouth knows too much about what my brain intends.

"That's generous," Hannah said approvingly. "Thank you, Liz."

Scarlatti smiled. "I think you've made the wisest choice, Ms. Sullivan. If you don't want media scrutiny, at any rate. Because pressing charges against a celebrity is a good way to get stuff splashed all over the papers."

"Speaking of the press, will you be issuing a statement?" Hannah gave Scarlatti a steely look. "After all, you were the ones who led them to believe that something untoward happened."

"Something untoward, as you say, did happen." Scarlatti was made of sterner stuff than to buckle at this juncture. "You were lucky to escape death. Is that what you want me to say?"

"Not at all." Hannah was a master at backpedaling. "I merely wondered if you would tell them that no charges will be filed, no crime was committed, and the death was accidental."

"Thank you for writing the script." Scarlatti gave an ironic bow. "We'll be making a statement to the press, as it happens."

"Speaking of a statement," I said, feeling as if I'd somehow gotten short shrift through my own stupid readiness to let go of my grievances, "I'd like to point out that I've been branded as an abductor and ex-con all across the nation. I will find it hard to get temp work, and the only writing assignments anyone will want to give me will involve dishing dirt on you, Hannah. 'The untold story of my terror ride with Hannah Couch.' That sort of thing."

Hannah exchanged glances with Richard Kendall. "I don't agree that my client is totally to blame for this situation, Ms. Sullivan," he said smoothly, "but of course she wouldn't want anyone to suffer through her actions, no matter how innocent they might have been. I'm sure we can come to some reasonable settlement."

"I don't want a settlement," I said, beginning to get steamed. "I want Hannah to announce to the world that no kidnapping occurred on my part, and she was in complete control the whole time. It's the truth. I know she believes in the truth."

Hannah sighed. "You're right, Liz. I do believe in the truth. But you don't understand the consequences. I'm not just me, Hannah Couch. I'm a whole corporate empire."

"Well, your whole corporate empire can apologize to me on national TV, or kiss my ass in court."

"Children, please don't quarrel yet." Scarlatti smiled around at us all. "Wait until we leave the room. And turn on your TV set. I guarantee, our sound bites will be on every network." She looked at Hannah. "They'll be after you like vultures. And you've lost your pit bull person who used to protect you, haven't you? Do you want to come down and make a statement with us? We can have an officer escort you back up afterward."

"That might be best." Hannah hesitated, then stepped forward and hugged me. I couldn't have been more surprised. "I am sorry if I impinged on your life, Liz. That was truly thoughtless. I have . . . I had a habit of riding roughshod over people who didn't seem important to my business. You've helped me see the fault in my behavior. I'll try to do right by you. I promise."

She sailed out of the room after Scarlatti and Daly. Richard Kendall paused to say to me, "I don't advise you to write anything for the tabloids, Ms. Sullivan. It might be considered actionable."

After they left, I turned to Kim and passed the hug to her. "We knew you would be okay."

"I don't feel okay," Kim said wanly. "They really put me through the wringer. I thought they were going to charge me with second-degree murder."

"They just say that to make you talk." I ignored Drake's snort of laughter.

"That's what Mr. Kendall said. He was very nice, really. He also said Hannah won't do the rest of the tour, at least not now. Maybe in a few months, when the furor has died down." Kim shivered. "I'm so glad. I just want to get home."

"I think we all feel like that. I know I do." I looked at my stalwart police companions. "Can we leave yet?"

"Don't you want to see Hannah on the news?"

"Not really." I went over to the library desk, found Judi Kershay's cell phone number in my knapsack, and dialed, while Don opened the doors of what I had thought was an antique armoire to reveal a huge TV. He turned it on and changed through the channels.

Judi came on the line. "Hi," I said. "It's your most troublesome temp worker."

"What's the latest?" She sounded worried. "I've been thinking about all of you."

"Well, the latest is, no one's arrested. Naomi's death was the result of an accident. And Hannah's canceling the tour."

"That would be best." Judi sounded relieved.

"I guess they're going to be leaving. Will the publisher make arrangements?"

"I'm sure they will." Judi hesitated. "Look, if Hannah wants me to, I'll clean up the loose ends for her. But then that's the end of our association."

"She's changed, I think." I stared at the TV screen. Don had found an all-news cable station, and they were doing a live feed from the hotel lobby downstairs. Flanked by the two police inspectors, Hannah began to speak. "Hold on. She's on TV. I have to hear this."

"I want to see it too. Call me later, or tell her to call me," Judi said. She hung up.

Mesmerized, all of us moved closer to the TV. A forest of microphones, a cacophony of shouted questions, greeted Hannah. The front steps of the hotel appeared to be rendered impassable by the phalanx of news people we'd avoided earlier by being brought up in the service elevator.

Hannah raised her hand to quiet the jackals of the press. Richard Kendall stood at her shoulder. As usual, she looked totally in command, although, without the special makeup, washed-out and pale. "As you can see, I am fine. Thank you for your concern. The unexpected death of my close associate Naomi Matthews overset me this morning, and I insisted that my driver get me away. She did not constrain me at all; I'm afraid the shoe was on the other foot. She very kindly drove me around until I could regain my composure, at which point we returned."

More shouted questions. "Where is she? How did Ms. Matthews die? Were you kidnapped?"

"I've explained that no abduction occurred, and no charged have been filed. The police will answer your further queries." Hannah stepped back and, despite the surging microphones, managed to get back into the hotel. The camera switched to Scarlatti, looking very mediagenic with her long blond hair. Next to her, Daly seemed pale.

"As Ms. Couch said, we have determined that Ms. Matthews died from accidental causes, and we are closing the case." Scarlatti smiled at the cameras. "As far as the supposed abduction is concerned, Ms. Couch has explained that to our satisfaction, and her driver, Elizabeth Sullivan, has declined to press charges."

This occasioned another barrage of yapping. I wondered how Hannah would like that.

Kim squeezed my arm. "I'm so glad, Liz."

Don shook my hand. "Way to go." He smiled at Kim. "I was wondering if you would mind me flying back to

Boston with you. I scheduled all this time for the tour, so I've got nothing on for the next few days."

"That would be nice." Kim's face glowed. "I'll love introducing you to Mom and Dad and everyone. They'll all be so surprised."

"As long as they don't hate me."

Her smile faded. "They won't hate you. But it may be hard for them to hear about Uncle Tony. You being there will make a good distraction."

Hannah came back into the suite, followed by Officer Diaz. "That was most unpleasant," she said with masterly understatement, "but at least it's over."

"I let Judi Kershay know you're canceling the rest of the tour."

"Thank you. I won't be sorry to get home and get away from all this." A shadow crossed her expression. "Poor Naomi. I will really miss her when I have time to think about it."

"Judi offered to tie up any loose ends for you if you want." I gave Hannah the piece of paper with Judi's number on it. "And I'm out of here."

Hannah offered me her hand. "You're a trouper, Liz. I thank you for your patience. If you're ever on the East Coast, let me know."

"Right." I did not add that it would be a cold day in hell before I'd look her up. I think we both knew that. And I extended no reciprocal invitation, no matter how impolite that might be.

Drake and Bruno shook hands all around. Kim came to give me one last hug. "Thanks," she whispered. "Thanks for holding on to me. I'm glad I didn't jump. I must have been crazy." Her face was red.

225

"We all get crazy sometimes." I wrote down my address for her. "Listen, let me know how it goes. I'm curious how Don feels about his new relatives."

She promised she would, and then we left. I was ready for bed. Especially if it was Drake's bed.

23

IT had been a long day of skiing, and I was tired. The snow was soft and wet, typical of March. I had never skied before, but Drake had persuaded me to go away with him for a long weekend at Lake Tahoe, and since I knew he needed a vacation after a couple of intense cases, I had agreed.

"You did very well for someone who's rusty," he said, only slightly condescending.

"Rusty, hell. I've never been on skis before in my life." I stretched my feet to the fire he'd built in the fireplace. The little log cabin he'd rented had won my heart when he'd pulled up in front of it the previous evening. It was near the Homewood ski area, amongst other cabins scattered under the snow-laden branches of tall sugar pines.

I had driven through Truckee on I-80, but never gotten into Tahoe. The beauty of the lake was overwhelming, and the quaint, alpine ambience had an undeniable appeal. Despite being a Colorado girl, I had never been able to afford trips to the mountains in the winter. Skiing was expensive, and my family was poor. I had been horrified at the amount Drake had shelled out that day for lift tickets, ski rentals, and snacks in the lodge.

"You wouldn't lie to me, would you?" He stretched out beside me on the couch. "The way you took those turns, I could swear you knew what you were doing."

"I listened to the instructor this morning. That's all."

"And you're short," he said, pulling me closer to him on the couch. "That helps."

We watched the flames contentedly, and then I went to the kitchen to make hot chocolate with a tot of brandy in it, according to Drake's instructions. He flipped lazily through the TV channels.

"Hey," he called. "Here's your friend."

I lowered the heat on the pan of milk and went to see what he was talking about. On the screen, Hannah Couch was showing how to pipe filling into deviled eggs.

"Thank goodness someone else has to be at her beck and call." I lingered, listening to the autocratic way she explained the only method worth using.

"Didn't she give you some money or something?"

"Yeah." She'd sent me a check, quite a generous one, to make up for any loss of income, the card had said. I thought of donating it to some worthy cause. In the end, I bought my vagrant pal Old Mackie some warm socks, and passed a chunk along to the Urban Ministry, but I kept the rest. My property taxes are a pretty worthy cause too.

"She's a piece of work, all right." Drake sniffed. "Is that milk boiling?"

He went into the kitchen to see to the hot chocolate—I had known he would at some point, because he cares about making it the right way, like Hannah cares about that, and as far as cooking goes, I don't care.

I stayed in front of the TV, watching Hannah arrange the deviled eggs on a special plate she had decorated herself (and you could too). I was about to change the channel when she went over to some windows and gestured gracefully at the curtains.

"A fun idea," she said, smiling at the camera with animation, "is to use old tablecloths to make curtains for your kitchen windows. The bright colors and patterns of vintage linens really complement a kitchen with collectibles in it. I like to display my salt cellars and old tin match holders."

I couldn't help myself. I started laughing.

"What's so funny?" Drake called over the counter that separated the tiny kitchen from the small living room.

"Nothing. Nothing, really. Turns out I earned that check Hannah sent."

"Every penny." He brought in the cups. Hot chocolate was good with brandy in it.

"You know," Drake said, turning off the TV, "they have wedding chapels in South Lake Tahoe."

"Is that so?" I waited for the familiar internal alarms to go off, but they didn't. Maybe because I was so pleasantly tired. Maybe because of the brandy.

"Yep. You can get married in half an hour. No muss, no fuss."

"No friends, no family." I met his smiling eyes. "That has a lot of appeal."

He stilled. "You mean, you'd actually consider—"

I took his face between my palms and kissed him. "Not this trip, mate. I need some time to really get used to the idea. But maybe next time, I'll ask you to Tahoe. And I'll bring along some rice."

Don't miss the earlier Liz Sullivan mysteries!

MURDER IN A NICE NEIGHBORHOOD
by Lora Roberts

While vagabond writer Liz Sullivan lies innocently sleeping in her '69 VW microbus, someone parks a dead body under it. The victim was a vagrant with whom Liz shared some unpleasant words just hours before the murder.

Setup? Maybe. But the police figure they've got their woman—unless she can provide them with a better alternative . . .

Published by Fawcett Books.
Available in your local bookstore.

MURDER IN
THE MARKETPLACE
by Lora Roberts

Freelance writer Liz Sullivan is on the scene when the body of beautiful Jenifer Paston is discovered. Jenifer happened to be a star at SoftWrite, the Silicon Valley company where Liz is temping.

Unfortunately, freelance writing doesn't always pay the bills—so Liz is forced to continue working at SoftWrite, where spite, sex, and greed take top priority, and where the computer games are murder.

Published by Fawcett Books.
Available at your local bookstore.

MURDER MILE HIGH
by Lora Roberts

For the first time in years, struggling writer Liz Sullivan is headed home to Denver to visit her estranged family. No sooner does she arrive than her former husband's corpse is delivered to her father's front porch with a bullet between the eyes.

Since Liz once tried to kill her violently abusive husband, the police assume she has finally succeeded. . . .

Published by Fawcett Books.
Available at your local bookstore.

MURDER BONE BY BONE
by Lora Roberts

Liz Sullivan is astonished when the two boys she is babysitting dig up human bones from the sidewalk under construction in front of the house.

Whose bones? Positive identification seems unlikely, but they appear to have been stashed away some thirty years ago. Liz and her friend, police detective Paul Drake, begin to ask questions—and they resurrect a past that would drive someone to murder in order to keep it buried.

Published by Fawcett Books.
Available at your local bookstore.

MURDER CROPS UP
by Lora Roberts

In the cheerful community garden where struggling freelance writer Liz Sullivan grows her veggies, someone is raking up old, hurtful scandals. So when a dead body turns up in nosy Lois Humphries's meticulously maintained plot, Liz is labeled a murderer.

Liz has a hard row to hoe—until she digs up dirt on some fellow gardeners who seem more than capable of giving the grim reaper a hand. . . .

Published by Fawcett Books.
Available in your local bookstore.